Jeff Galloway

Return of the Tribes
to Peachtree Street

Library of Congress Cataloging in Publication Data

Galloway, Jeff, 1945-
Return of the Tribes to Peachtree Street

1. Running. 2. Running-Training. 3. Fitness-Health. I. Title.

ISBN: 0-964-71870-7

We are grateful to the following photographers for permission to reprint their photos on the cover:

>   *Marathon Foto*
>   *Jeff Johnson*
>   *Peachtree Road Race Magazine*

First Printing: June 1995

Printed in the United States of America

Phidippides Publication
PO Box 76843
Atlanta GA 30358 USA

TABLE OF CONTENTS

....

FIRST STEPS....THE SILENT REVOLUTION

1

*A*s this is an interactive book in progress, I welcome your input. It is the sharing of information, experience and some of ourselves that makes exercise one of the gentle and significant molders of our lives. Please fill out the form at the end of this book, and return it. I'd love to read your ideas and suggestions.

has migrated out of the stands and on to the playing field. This produced the quickest dramatic change to better health in American history. But while this groundswell response anticipates health trends of the 21st century, individuals also report the satisfaction of expressing primitive, hidden instincts to use leg and back muscles to move forward, and to migrate towards something greater than the sum of the energy of the individual participants. Indeed, the countless long distance walk/runs of our ancestors were necessary for survival, and the large folk fitness events hook us into this heritage.

This book is dedicated to the millions of heroes who gave up comfortable, secure, sedentary life-styles, and decided to put themselves to the test. Many did this without support; indeed, many received negative reinforcement from normally well-meaning friends, co-workers and family members. Out of the struggle, however, emerged a new person, with capabilities not imagined before.

A few did this alone. But many more have joined groups of 2 or more and added the chemistry of their personalities to the mix of energy and inspiration. In this way, the process became fun. They learned some good jokes and a lot of bad ones. The soap opera which is everyone's life opens up more during exercise as people speak directly from the heart.

Starting in the late 70's a significant and growing percentage of the US population

The positive impact of this revolution has only started. As more enjoy the fun of migrations like the Peachtree Road Race, and corporate health promotions like the Office Depot Run/Walk and Company Picnic, a greater percentage of those who start, continue. A powerful trend is the satisfaction of taking responsibility for one's own health. The result is a mass enrollment in the most successful healthcare system on earth, which promises to reduce costs more than medication or high-tech equipment combined.

But today's life-style exercisers don't continue to get out there just because it's healthy. *Once into the activity, partici-pants discover that they are more active in other areas of life, and mentally more alert. But many wouldn't roll out of bed on the difficult, early mornings unless the group was waiting. And all find a won-derful sense of satisfaction in helping one another on those days when a gentle push from one spirit to another is needed and silently appreciated.*

The characters you'll meet in the follow-ing pages are not specific people, but they share the problems and hidden strengths of us all. Like all of us, they let their lives become cluttered and over-committed. The simple, liberating act of lifting oneself off the ground provided the catalyst for making many connections inside, which produced positive changes in many other areas of life.

But the main goal is the fun that occurs when we exert ourselves correctly. It is the purpose of this book to help make every one of your exertions enjoyable. I'm proud to say that most of my runs today are slower, but they are more fun. We are programmed for exertion. Our bodies and minds reward us in many ways when we do it correctly.

So lets give into our primitive instincts on a regular basis and find a good migration!

BEFORE YOU GET STARTED.....

There are very few people who should not exercise because of cardiovascular, structural, muscular, or other problems. It is very important to ensure that you are not in this risk category.

- Before beginning any exercise, diet or other improvement program, be sure to have yourself and the program evaluated by specialists in the areas you are pursuing.

- The advice in this book is offered as such—advice from one exerciser to another. It is not meant to be a prescription and should be evaluated as noted above and below.

- Specific structures and problems of individuals may require program modifications.

- Try to find specialists who are knowledgeable about their area and the effects of exercise.

- Ask several respected leaders in the fitness community for recommendations of specialists.

- Always back off any exercise or program when you feel any risk of injury or health.

- The benefits come from regular exercise and steady adherence to a long-term program.

- Joining a group helps motivation.

- Have FUN and you'll want to continue.

4

*S*aturday,
March 5
"Olympic
Stadium is in
sight, and the lead group
has been reduced to 2.
Nackahara of Japan is
running within himself,
and closing the gap on
Waihuri of Kenya. It
looks like a great race is
shaping up—wait—a
third runner is closing
the gap. Who is that
skinny guy?

apologized and started
to find another seat, but
noticed that his table-
mate was wearing a
familiar sweatshirt.

"So you went to the
Wyndham reunion this
weekend—I'm Tom
Burke"

"Sam Gladstone, one of
the more ancient
classes, celebrating (I
guess) 30 years." Both
listened as the airport
announcer said "For those going on
PlaneValue Airlines flight number 99—
that flight will be delayed until we can
get a plane in here—about 1am. We
appologize for any inconvenience."

He had been strolling, bored, down the
commuter airline concourse at Logan
International Airport, munching on a
soft pretzel. Turning sharply upon
hearing the commentary on the Sports
Channel of the **Home Depot Atlanta
International 5K**, the pretzel eater
stopped and watched the bar's TV from
the concourse. But the next action shot
had him glued to the set as he moved
toward the chairs near the screen.

"That's Tim Kennedy, a hometown
boy—let's see if he can enter the tough
world of international distance running"

As the local guy passed the Japanese
runner and took on the Kenyan, the
pretzel-eater dropped his pretzel, and
grabbed the first empty chair in the bar
area, unconsciously knocking over the
carry-on bag of the fellow reading a
book at the table he had invaded. At the
commercial break, the pretzel eater

You could feel a cumulative groan from
dozens who had filled up the seating in
the gate area and had spilled out into the
aisle. Bodies were sprawled everywhere,
trying to get some rest.

"They always apologize," said Tom.

Tom noted that the Atlanta flight would
be the last flight out of Logan that night.
He added: "I've spent the night in some
of the world's most efficient airports
while trying to fly this airline, it never
gets any easier when you go for the best
price." Sam noted that he had an important but negative-oriented meeting with
his boss the next morning and didn't like
the prospect that he was going to be very
tired.

When the road race show resumed, Tom explained that the coverage was from an event he had attended, **The Home Depot Atlanta International**. The veteran Kenyan seemed to have the young Georgian under his control, but as the camera zoomed in, one could tell that both athletes were pushing one another to the limit. Great, up-close camera work displayed the honesty of every effort they didn't want to make in an attempt to break away from the other, and the resulting disappointment when the tactic didn't work.

"See, the African in second, he may have lost it when he accelerated so hard. Kennedy still has the fire in his eyes."

As if to prove him wrong, the second place runner struggled past his competitor and burst to a quick 10 meter lead.

"Now watch," said Tom, "the original leader will get it back together and take command."

But it wasn't that easy for the young Atlantan who struggled against the African. On the straining faces, a tactical poker game played out during the last few hundred yards of this competitive race. The slight, non-muscular runner who was now behind, was under duress, and could have easily given in to the challenge. Instead he dug down once and accelerated. His competitor in green, responded, and the muscle definition seemed to give the edge to him. The skinny guy with the red stripe on his shirt betrayed his feelings, and showed an "I might as well give up" look but grimaced and responded again, and the effort was easily met by his competitor. As they entered

the final turn, both were running as fast as they could run, and Kennedy seemed to be giving in a little to the strong surges by the more athletic opponent when Tom, who couldn't help himself, shouted, "Don't give up, Tim," attracting attention up and down the concourse. "You're smoother than he is. You'll get him." And he did. The courageous young runner seemed to find a new source of energy as he smoothly increased his turnover rate, wearing on his strained face the satisfaction of knowing there was nothing left to give. But the runner in green had too much ability, far more racing experience, and pulled away just before the finish line. The crowd, which had now gathered around the TV, buzzed with response and then dispersed as the TV show went into another commercial break.

"You guessed wrong, but just barely. I'm impressed," noted Sam, "or is this a rerun which you've seen before?"

"No, I used to make it my business to read the signs in runners' faces. I knew the kid who finished second. He used to run against my boy 9 years ago, when he was a soccer player. That kid has heart and he has developed about the smoothest running form I've seen.

"And for those of you in Atlanta," the TV announcer broke in, "this is the magic month for getting your entry into the Peachtree Road Race. In just over two weeks, on the day the entry forms are printed, all of the issues of the Atlanta newspapers will be gone from the news stands, within a 24 hour period, as an estimated 100,000 clip their coupons and hope that the US mail delivers their entry in time to become one of the 'only' 50,000 who are selected to enter and win the coveted Peachtree Road Race T-shirt."

"I walk down to watch the finish each year," said Sam, "and I'm always amazed at how many of the finishers—including many who finish under 50 minutes—look as overweight as I am. What a joy it is to see the expressions on their faces; pain, satisfaction, exhilaration, and mostly the glow of accomplishment."

When the waitress came over, Tom noted that they still had an hour before the Atlanta flight, and they decided to buy a drink.

They started to talk about the weekend. Neither Tom nor Sam could explain why they went to the reunion.

"I've been trying to articulate why, after being away so long, I chose this reunion to make my very first visit back to the school. I feel that I'm trying to regain some of the energy and excitement I felt during my last 2 years at Wyndham, and throughout my graduate studies. You see, Tom, I've had tenure at Georgia International University for 20 years, I'm secure as one can be in this age in my job, I have a comfortable income, but feel that I'm missing something, some spark to get the energy flowing again. I keep having this sinking feeling that the world is losing it's "fiber"—the moral underpinnings—or am I losing my own. Maybe I should take a stand, especially when the university takes away a beloved project I believe in, but I don't any more.

"I have similar feelings." agreed Tom. "So much of my identity used to be determined by my image of myself as an athlete. When that went away, I've felt a void. I used to stand for something."

"Maybe we're talking about perception," observed Sam. "As a student I realized the questions, the issues of life that I couldn't answer. But I believed that I'd have a handle on some of these by now, but I don't."

"Yea," agreed Tom. "I came to a similar realization this weekend. When I graduated, I accepted the fact that I didn't have the knowledge or experience to confront the big questions, but assumed that I would. Now I admit that there are no answers for most of these. But what bothers me is that this realization doesn't bother me. I used to engage my inner spirit by pushing against the unknown. Now I feel that I'm becoming too "mushy."

Tom asked if the cigarette smoke from a nearby booth bothered him, and Sam said he could cope with it. Tom waved the stream coming from a nearby table as he listened to the enjoyable philosophical story of this gentle professor of Anthropology who was coming to the end of a 10 year grant studying the migration habits of early man. "I've finished everything but the conclusion, which shouldn't take much longer. I've secured funding to finish it, but I feel that my new Dean doesn't want to renew it."

Unlike Sam, Tom had struggled hard at Wydham to keep his grades up while he trained and competed for the Cross

Country and Track teams. In spite of this great academic challenge, Tom realized that the rigors of this academic institution had forced him to learn how to think and to strip away layers of superficial and conflicting information to analyze the issues. This had ultimately helped his professional life in many positive ways. While he was proud that his education had given him a head start, he had to admit, with a feeling of some insecurity, that this didn't seem to help him now.

As the credits ended the roadrace show, Sam watched the pack come in. Half of the runners were over 40, many overweight.

"The running craze interests me," Sam said. "This weekend I was hoping to find a sign that others my age are finding the spark, but I only met four. As I tried to find the similarities among them, and the differences with the others, there were only 2 factors which immediately appeared: all had shifted into new careers, about 5 years ago, and all now run marathons after having been sedentary for years."

After Tom was half way into his second Busch, he started to open up a bit, and to attack the smoking industry.

"You know, Sam, the smoke from that booth over there really bothers me. I really hope that those two big lawsuits against the big tobacco companies bring them to their knees.

Sam didn't say much at first and then countered with an argument expected from a North Carolina native. "You must

realize that my father and grandfather were tobacco farmers, but it seems that individuals at some point must take responsibility for their own actions."

"Yea, the healthy have to pay for the habit that is promoted heavily by the tobacco companies. This habit gets people addicted, and leaves the medical bills to the family of the victims, and to the taxpayers."

Sam changed the subject by asking Tom about his running background.

"For me, running was a mixed bag. On the flight up here from Atlanta, I told myself that I wasn't trying to 'find myself' or gain a new direction, but maybe I have at least figured out how I got misdirected earlier. Possibly one of the negative sides of this liberal arts education is just too much freedom and the belief that almost anything is possible. I didn't focus enough on the key word 'almost'."

Tom noted how, upon graduation, he had obsessively pursued an unsuccessful dream to make the Olympic team. "Graduation, marriage and parenthood came too quickly. I wasn't ready. So I guess I withdrew into my dream to avoid dealing with the reality that I didn't want and the problems that resulted from my retreat."

"It's interesting that you feel you're missing something, Sam. On New Year's eve I was in an unusually reflective mood and confronted the reality that I really don't know my son. He is just about the age I was when I graduated from Wyndham. I've gotta tell you that I had several flashbacks this weekend—thinking about some of the things I went through 20 years ago—and wondering what my son is going through. He probably thinks his dad is a drifter and not very responsible, and he's not wrong.

Tom wondered why he was telling this to a stranger. He'd never confessed this to anyone. Maybe it was the professorial confidence which Sam exuded, or maybe it was the shared and somewhat cozy experience at Wyndham. Tom felt comfortable talking to Sam.

"You'd be surprised," said Sam. "Often the characteristics of the other parent, which the primary caregiver wants to eliminate from the offspring, become very intriguing to the offspring.

"I hope that you're wrong on that one, professor. I didn't use good judgement when I was 22. I realized this weekend that I miss the focus I had when I was working out with the guys, and the feeling that I was headed toward something positive, my Olympic dream. I *stood for something* then, I had some 'fiber'. This weekend, some of those who were on the track team 20 years ago got together for a grudge match—and the good feelings came back—the mental focus, the extra energy, the joking around—the fun. But the run quickly showed me how out of shape I've gotten during the past 2 years. The mind remembers and the muscles don't."

They moved their discussion to the departure gate, where they grabbed a boarding pass designating their numeri-cal order in choosing a seat. When their numbers were called, several other passengers rushed in front of them, and others pushed their way ahead. "Reminds me of a cattle drive," observed Sam.

"This airline never has a proceedure for lining up. It's survival of the rudest," observed Tom.

Just as they got to the 4th row, three friends decided to move back to join their buddies, and Sam and Tom quickly took the aisle and window seats.

Tom then said, "Sam, tell me why you're losing that research project."

"Our institution is struggling financially. We're going through the pains of transition to a new president with a new philosophy. The new man is the first businessman to assume that position—and is upsetting the academic apple cart by hiring new people. They think they can run a university like a business. There's lot's of uncertainty. There is a major move away from research toward the teaching of large lecture classes."

Tom could read the stress, Sam's face and neck muscles. He fully expected Sam to change the subject, and he did. "So, Tom, you were a candidate for the Olympics?" Sam's voice was filled with respect.

"I dreamed that I had a shot in 1980. It really wasn't that glamorous. I just put my life on hold. I trained and took a few part-time jobs. After 3 years of supporting us by waiting on tables, seeing my friends with secure careers, my wife, pregnant told me to get a job. After all of that, the US decided to boycott those Moscow games. I felt like a fool, and the whole situation put a final stress on our marriage. The only bright spot at that time was my job, working for an idealist who opened a running store. Unfortunately it went bankrupt."

"It seems that with so many people running, that should be a good business." observed Sam.

"The running shoe business is quite strong, but many runners go for the lowest price in catalogs and discount stores. When the store dies due to loss of business, the same runners are frustrated by not having a shoe expert around to keep them from accumulating a closet full of bargains which don't fit, or aren't designed for their feet. Suddenly there's no place to buy the specialty items which make running more interesting. The price difference is often only a few dollars, or the same price. It's the perception of lower prices which fuels the discount buying and kills the specialty store. There aren't many of the true 'service' stores left."

Tom continued to relate that as his marriage faltered due to financial problems, he was hired another visionary who set up worksite health promotion programs for businesses in an attempt to get the insurance companies to lower their rates because healthy people would file fewer claims.

"I guess there weren't enough people with healthy foresight in decision-making positions to make it work, so our company took on new leaders, and a new direction. Now, with a re-organized version of the same business, I manage special events for businesses, which range in complexity from getting clowns to company office parties to planning company picnics for 6,000."

"Suppose you had gotten a good job and given up your pursuit of the dream. Would your marriage have lasted?" asked Sam.

"No, we were on different levels. We didn't communicate. She had no consciousness of what it was like to be an athlete pursuing internal goals. To her credit, she has pursued a successful career as a manager in the medical field. She moved to Pensacola 8 years ago, and I haven't seen much of my son since.

Before he had a chance to continue, the stand-by's boarded, looking for the "leftovers." At the very end of the line was a woman who seemed particularly relaxed and unhurried as she made her way down the aisle. The flight attendant closed the door, and the standard announcement began: "The pilot cannot move the aircraft until all passengers are seated with their seatbelts securely fastened." She came to Sam and Tom's row and realized, that the announcement was directed at her. She quickly picked the seat between them, stuffed miscellaneous clothing back into her bag and stowed it in front of her. She pulled a sheet of wrinkled paper from her purse, and started writing. The flight attendant, a very young looking muscular male noticed her bag and said:

"I'm sorry Miss, but the bag must be completely beneath the seat in front of you."

"You're kidding, aren't you?" she replied. "It's sticking out an inch and a half."

At this threat to his authority, the flight attendant's muscles seemed to puff up a bit as he told her that he was empowered to ensure the safety of all those on the plane. "Nothing can stick out, not even a fraction of an inch."

"You mean you're going to make a big deal over that?"

"It's in the regulations. Want to see them?"

"No, I'll just stuff it," she said, as she pushed by Tom into the aisle and took her time spreading out her garments in various overhead compartments. The flight attendant looked on, and wanted to hurry her up. As she finished, the flight attendant said his sterile "Thank You." She looked him straight in the eye and said "This is the last flight I will ever take on PlaneValue airlines."

"If you don't take a space, someone else will," he replied.

"I've only heard that line from flight attendants on two other airlines, People's Express and Eastern," she added, looking him straight in the eyes again.

Sam tried to take the edge off the scene by continuing the Peachtree conversation. "I've thought about trying the outing on July 4th many times, but it seemed to be too much work. I started walking about a year ago, thinking I might go to this reunion. I guess I secretly feared that those who returned

would be almost as lean and youthful looking as when I last saw them, but most were as overweight and as limited in endurance as I. I am not aware of what it takes to be dedicated. The best I can say is that I can cover the 3 mile loop around Chastain Park in less than an hour, on a good day. But I struggle. I haven't been feeling good on my walks during the past few weeks—I just can't imagine how someone would keep going for over 6 miles—at my age."

The flight attendant told the young woman to put up her serving tray, which caused only a mild look of irritation. As she continued to scribble on the paper, Tom seemed to recognize the color and shape of the form—and inquired,

"Isn't that the Peachtree Road Race application from the Atlanta Track Club?"

"Yea, I brought this up to my former man friend, who's a runner, and he just told me that he won't be needing it, and also won't be needing me."

Not knowing how to follow that comment, Tom continued with his running theme. "Yea, I used to be a member of the ATC because they give members a head start on entering the Peachtree Road Race. Did your friend come down from Boston each year to run with you?"

The woman laughed. "No, No, HE was the runner and he *used* to live in Atlanta. Running was always a bone of contention in our relationship. I tried to put up with the long weekend morning runs, the stress relievers he called them, in the evenings after work. I even went with him to a running vacation last summer. I never ran but did pick up some good information about fat burning, foods, and mental attitude. He had a good job in Atlanta but was always complaining about the hours, or the boss. He moved back home to work in his family's grocery store—at a great reduction in pay—so he could concentrate on his running. The man is 40 and he's not going to win the Peachtree—I should have told him to get a life much earlier—now he told me."

Tom wasn't sure he wanted to ask the question, but he did anyway. "So you came up to visit, or just to deliver his Peachtree stuff?"

Tom enjoyed the young woman's reaction to the slightly embarrassing comments. She hesitated, trying to pick the right thing to say and then spoke with a "what does it matter anyway" air.

"I wanted to continue the relationship, and he didn't. I'm OK with it. He could have waited a year before telling me. Just after he told me he wanted to split, he gave me all the motivation I'll ever need to do this 'Peachtree' thing," she said, waving the application in the air. "When I said I was thinking about entering he had the nerve to tell me that I'd never do it, so I will."

"I suppose you've run it before, Tom?" asked Sam.

"Yea, I was even thinking about entering this year. It's the 25th anniversary of my first race. But I keep remembering the psychological scars and my disappointment years ago. Running used to hurt

because of the speedwork I did almost every day. Now, I can't imagine going back to it when my life is so crowded with everything else."

The First Peachtree Road Race—1970

Enrollment: 110
% of women: less than 1%
Average Age: @ 20
Start: Peachtree and West Paces Ferry
Staging for the Start: parking lot of the Buckhead Sears store
Finish: Peachtree at the Equitable Bldg (just north of 5 points)
T shirt: No
Biggest reward at finish: a dip in the Equitable fountain
% of field known by average participant: @95%

The middle passenger turned to Sam and introduced herself. "Hi, I'm Suzi Baker. I realize that you two have probably discussed this, but, do you run?"

"I'm Sam, Suzi, and I only teach about running, in an indirect way. I conduct research about ancient peoples who migrated thousands of miles in their lifetimes, but I only let my fingers run over the keyboard of my computer. I actually tried running about 8 years ago and my wife convinced me that I'm so overweight and out of shape that I'd probably have a heart attack. At my age, people may think about changing things, like getting into exercise, but they don't."

"Tell me about it. I work with people who are always trying," said Suzi.

"But I'm one of the great majority," continued Sam, "who don't do anything about it, except take a nice walk 2-3 times a week. Now Tom over there used to train for the Olympics."

Suzi turned to Tom, and realized that this was the opportunity she had to make him squirm. She asked, "Pardon my look of amazement, but I thought that runners were supposed to be thin."

Without showing his defensiveness about being overweight, Tom looked thoughtful. "Sam and I just watched a great race on television, which caused me to think. About every 2-3 years I've tried to get back into running, but during the past 2 years, I've done nothing. Maybe it's time for a comeback. You know, I miss it. I miss the dedication, the 'mission', the sense of having a positive anchor to my lifestyle. During my run—that was the only time I really felt that I was in control—I consistently felt good about myself. But I know, at 42, I'm not going to ever run as fast as I did before, so what's the point?"

"Tell me about your research," Suzi asked Sam.

"I'm finding that there may be some basic, biological reason why Tom feels 'in control' when he runs. Man evolved as a running/walking animal. He designed himself to be an efficient endurance animal, in order to survive. To cover the distances most efficiently, the exercise mode was a mixture of walking and running. Short running segments were infused regularly into the walking. The more urgent the need to migrate, the more often the insertion. It was com-monplace for ancient man to cover extremely long distances in order to gather meager food supplies and to avoid predators. We are creatures designed for forward movement and cardiovascular activity."

"And we receive pleasure—physically and psychologically—when we go back to these roots," added Suzi. "I've seen some recent research—"you see, I'm a psychologist, which shows that when people move forward, as in walking or running, they stimulate certain organizational centers of the brain. Walking starts the process, and some running seems to increase the ability of the brain to 'format' itself, to organize itself by straightening out mental tasks, setting priorities, etc. Most interesting is that brain activity is localized around the section needed for creative thought and, on the other side, clear logical thinking. Both areas are separated by a wall and don't interact, but running and walking stimulated both sides simultaneously in the 'productive' areas. On the other hand, the areas of the brain which tend to have neuroses and psychoses are cut off for an extended time after exercise. My guess is that walking and running together seem to stimulate some primitive mental processes which help to stabilize emotions and keep the exerciser away from the negative mental forces."

Suzi, went on. "Whatever the major project was, both for work and in other areas of their life, the research also noticed a definite increase in ability to keep problem-solving on track, and maintain a positive attitude among those who ran regularly."

Sam asked if there was a difference in the effect of walking vs. running. Suzi explained that those who walked and ran in regular intervals had about the same benefits as the runners. Walkers didn't receive as many benefits as runners, but were significantly better off than the control group.

"I've noticed a slight increase in my overall attitude when I'm walking regularly with my wife," said Sam.

"Six months later—and then one year later—the runners and the walk/runners showed an increased tendency to take responsibility for their health, and to some extent, to take responsibility for other problems and areas of their lives," noted Suzi.

"How was that measured?" asked Tom.

"In follow-up surveys of lifestyle health, and family surveys."

"I've concluded, from my studies," said Sam, "that the very ancient behavior of running has been such a necessary and basic part of the human existance—that we are rewarded when we do it in many physiological ways, mental relaxation, and release of endorphin pain-killers. I'd really love to do a little running, but when I tried before, I could only get up to half a mile without stopping. It hurt

My Favorite Things

	Sam	Suzi	Tom
Favorite Food/how often	Chicken Fried Steak/3x week	Veg pasta, white sauce/3x week	Big Mac/5x week
Exercise/how often	3 mi walk/2x week	5 min walk/4x week	1 hr basketball/1x wk
Leisure time	Read Newspaper	Read mysteries, shopping	TV—sports
What I will do in 10 years	Retired—looking for something	Same as now	Same as now
What I Hate	Nothing—that I know of	Watching Sports, execise	Shopping

so much I just lost interest. It's probably age."

"You were probably doing too much at one time, and you didn't practice what you preach," said Suzi.

Sam looked at her with a puzzled look.

"I got dragged into all of this by my former friend," said Suzi, "who took me to the Galloway running vacation in North Carolina last summer. The 'new' idea is called CRUISING—and it sounds like the same program followed by early man—run a little and walk a little. You don't even have to run, you can skip, bounce, jump or bound along. I tried it the week I was at Lake Junaluska and worked up to 2 miles, easily. Now I haven't done anything about it since, that is, until tomorrow.

Did you meet anyone my age," asked Sam, "who could get further than 2-3 miles without being totally exhausted?"

"I met several in the Galloway program last summer who couldn't run a step, 6-8 months before the NYC marathon. They not only did it, but had fun and wanted to do another. It almost got me interested in running. Even when I do the Peachtree, I'm going to *cruise* it, not *run* it."

Sam asked how these beginners arranged the walking and the running, and Suzi explained that beginners usually run only a minute and walk for two-three minutes, from the beginning of every session. For a moment, Sam's eyes seemed to say 'yes, that is do-able'. Then the oppressive force of reality set

in. "You've gotten me interested, but I'm still faced with the inertia of not having done anything physical for the last 20 years of my life."

"I've got another problem—and excuse—for not exercising," said Tom. "After 20 years of constant pounding, my body just broke down. Every year, for the past 3, I've tried to go back to running and have come down with an injury of some type, knee, achilles, plantar fascia, you name it."

When Suzi probed and found out that Tom had been running 5-6 days a week

---

Fitness Mistakes—which cause burnout

Sam:
1. Tried to run continuously for more than a half mile (should have run 1-2 min & walked 2 min)
2. Started out each run too hard—for him (should have started by shuffling slowly—with walks)
3. Told himself before each run that he was going to feel bad (should have forcast a fun, easy run)
4. Tried to exercise when blood sugar and motivation was low (should have eaten something first)

Tom:
1. Kept telling self that he was going to get injured (should have been positive—but sensitive to injury signs)
2. Tried to start with speed workouts he had done in his 20's (should have adjusted for age)
3. Ran too many days per week (after 35 years old—run 3-4 days per week)
4. Kept comparing self to times when he was in top shape (should have accepted current level—worked from there)

during his 'comeback' phases, she volunteered more advice.

"You're doing it all wrong. I learned this summer that even veteran athletes should run no more often than every other day when they're coming back from inactivity. Not only do you reduce injury and fatigue, you'll get fit quicker.

"For someone who is seemingly proud of never running before," said Sam, "you're suddenly the expert."

All three laughed and Suzi was instantly given the title of "coach."

Suzi explained that her former running friend made her take extensive notes at all of the Running Camp sessions, and she developed these into a manual. Much of the information which Galloway taught had been developed since he wrote his last book. She had typed it up as a Peachtree present under the title "Galloway's Guerrilla Guide." Tom asked if she had given it to him, and Suzi smiled a devilish smile and said, "No, and he'll never get it now!"

As the flight attendant delivered their meals, Sam declined and asked if they had something for indigestion. After dinner, Sam and Tom shared stories about the "reunion resolutions" which were made that weekend. Sam related how a fellow who had been divorced 3 times explained his new strategy; before he got married again, he was going to meet the woman's lawyer.

Tom told the success story of a fellow track team member who had studied to be a teacher and received a masters degree, and wasn't happy when he got into the classroom. He got a part-time job working in the mail room of an ad agency, and loved it. For 5 years he did almost everything in the business until he found his calling—creating ads. Today he designs ads for some of the biggest businesses in the world. "While it inspired me, it made me sick," joked Tom. "This guy runs more now than he did in college. Says he has to run to cope with the stress of deadlines and to get the creative juices flowing. It's not enough that he's rich and famous. He can beat me. I used to run circles around him."

After a while, Sam said he wasn't feeling good and tried to recline and rest. As the plane moved into position for landing Sam asked Tom and Suzi if they felt that the airplane had enough oxygen in it. He mentioned that he was having trouble breathing. Tom noticed that Sam's face was gray and strained. He called the flight attendant.

When the experienced woman arrived, she calmed everyone down, but Suzi and Tom knew that something was wrong. She left for a few minutes and returned with a senior flight attendant who left and made an announcement asking if there was a doctor on the plane. The original flight attendant stayed with Sam, reassuring him that this was just a precaution, and a doctor appeared to ask him some questions. Instead of going into a normal holding pattern, Tom noticed that their plane went right into the Hartsfield runway, and right to the gate. Passengers in the rows ahead of them were told to stay in their seats, and Sam was rolled out on a stretcher.

Tom didn't know why, but he wanted to be the support crew and accompany Sam to the hospital. He convinced the flight attendant that he was a close friend and went with him. The medical team at the gate, however, wouldn't let him go in the ambulance, but Tom found that they were taking him to the heart center at Peachtree Hospital. Suzi rushed up to him as the passengers poured off the plane and begged to go with him to check on Sam. They rushed into the West long-term parking lot without saying a word, picked up Tom's car and headed for the hospital.

Sam and Suzi waited for hours in the hospital. Sam's wife, Teresa, came in from time to time to report on the progress of the angioplasty operation that Sam was undergoing. A test had shown blockage of one of the primary arteries supplying the heart. The opera-tion brought a balloon-like instrument to the site, and enlarged the blocked area. Doctors had assured Teresa that even though there was great risk going into the heart, Sam had an excellent chance of coming through the operation.

About 3am, Suzi decided to go home and Tom walked her to the taxi. Both were amazed that they had stayed so long and felt so involved with someone who they only met a few hours before. When Tom found out the part of Mid-town where she lived, he insisted upon taking her home. Neither said a word as they walked across the quiet campus of Peachtree Hospital, during the deadest part of the night shift.

Just as they were leaving the hospital building, Suzi broke the silence. "I wonder what Sam will do with the rest of his life?"

Tom went back into the hospital to ask the name of Sam's doctor. The tired but pleasant attendant looked up Sam's record, very sleepily, and told him "Just ask for 'Dr. Life'. Everybody calls him that."

After the two hours of silence in the hospital, they suddenly couldn't stop.

"I feel like he needed me to be there," said Sam.

"There's a theory in social psychology," noted Suzi, "that any situation can set up a number of roles and expectations. Humans have the capacity to jump in and provide very caring behaviors even when they didn't know one another, in response to the needed role."

Tom mused, "It really makes you think, 'what's it all about'? "Here's a highly intelligent, highly educated man who was supported through his career by his University, producing significant research. Enter a new college president with a different set of priorities, and his project has no significance. He has to start over. This may not have had anything to do with the heart attack, but it makes me think, 'what lifetime projects are worthwhile'? What should I

be doing with my life?"

As if he sensed that things were getting too heavy, Tom added, "of course I probably won't change a thing, but it's interesting to think about it."

"But, I can identify," said Suzi. "Most of the time, I have no idea whether I help my clients or not. In some cases, I feel certain that I have set them back. I often feel that I should just start over, get into a field in which I can receive better feedback, and a better sense of helping people. I got into this psychology business to help people. They come to me and bear their souls, and I can't do a thing. I continually ask myself, 'is this what I want to do with the rest of my life'?"

"My boss took me aside last week," confided Tom, "and told me I was losing my focus. I started to get angry with him, but realized that there have been several incidents each week in which I've let deadlines slip, or failed to follow-up on routine things or projects I've done before. The woman I dated told me 6 months ago that I was losing my energy level. You know, they're right. What bothers me most is that I accept it. Three years ago, I wouldn't have let these things happen, or at least I would have counter-attacked, gotten the engines running again, if only to *show* them.

"Has there been a shift in company philosophy?" asked Suzi.

"The original owner of my company..." noted Tom.

"...You mean the visionary," asked Suzi.

"Yes, he hired me to set up wellness focus groups for corporations. We conducted about a dozen of these, began to get some good documentation, started to see some great breakthroughs in individuals, and the new boss cancels them because the profit is too small."

Suzi was interested in hearing more about this project. They drove up to her midtown duplex, parked, and continued their talk. Tom explained that these retreats took key executives—or rising stars—and brought them together for 3-7 days in a resort setting, away from the office. Usually, strategic planning issues were discussed, but Tom's job was to develop teamwork, through fitness activites which were fun. Regardless of starting level, there were activities for everyone, and every group said that the attitude and productivity of the session was as good or better than any confer-ence they had attended. Tom reported that most of the companies used their follow-up program to keep the partici-pants motivated. As he got into the particulars of this project, Tom felt better about himself, that he might still have the spark inside.

"Any follow-up studies?" asked Suzi.

"Yes, 93% were still exercising 6 months afterward, in the monitored programs. Several of the corporations used this to initiate health promotion programs which have reduced their insurance premiums significantly over the years. This is the type of cutting-edge project that our company should do to move healthcare ahead into the preventive arena.

Tom paused, and a sad sense of revela-tion came over his face as he continued.

"But even if my boss told me tomorrow to get a project together, look at me. How can I expect to lead others into a healthy lifestyle when I eat poorly, do almost no exercise, and carry around about 30 more pounds than I did 18 months ago? In 10 years I could be Sam, and not survive the heart attack. There is heart disease in my family."

They had reached a thoughtful impass, and both were very tired. They didn't want the evening to end, so they decided to walk around the park near Suzi's house and to talk about Suzi's attempt to do the Peachtree. As they passed her house the first time, Suzi noted a sparkle in Tom's eye when he related stories about the early days.

"What really pushed my button was the race we saw on TV in Boston. That kid who finished second showed such great courage. I want to bring back that sense of digging deep and finding the strength. It still bothers me that I won't be able to run the times I did when I was younger. But I need something to get the spark going. I want to be dedicated again. That wimpy kid should have given in. His competitor had run almost half a minute faster recently than the kid had run in his life. Every race has hundreds of stories of inspiration and courage. I'm inspired."

As they passed Suzi's place for the 4th time, she was ready to stop, but begged Tom to help her stay on her Peachtree training program. Tom decided that it was their mission to get Sam out and walking as soon as his doctor would allow it. Out of the raw honesty of her fatigue, Suzi looked Tom in the eye and told him very professionally, "you know that we are all able to make significant lifestyle changes, but very, very few of us actually do."

Tom got a little twinkle in his eye and replied, "Yea but we're not ordinary people, we've just become runners, we have a reason and a deadline, July 4th."

Suzi enjoyed the force of his positive counterattack. After a handshake, she went inside, and Tom went back to the hospital. Both felt better about themselves, and life itself, than they had in many months.

Just as the first light of dawn was glowing above a deserted Peachtree Street, Tom headed toward the Hospital, on an emotional rollercoaster. The physical and emotional fatigue didn't help as he hit a low, thinking about his loss of focus at work. He would climb out of the low with the thoughts of reviving the concepts of his company's founder, then go down again with guilt about not knowing or giving direction to his son. Each cycle had ended on an "up" note as he imagined himself

running again, and 20 pounds lighter.

As he watched the sun rise from the window of the Heart Center he hung onto his interest and support of Sam as a symbol that he cared. Such symbols were more important to him now than at any other time in his life.

A familiar nurse assured him that everything was going well, that Sam's wife had gone home, and that he should too. His mind shifted into fatigue gear # 5 as he gathered up some magazines and stumbled toward the door. Then he heard someone yell his name.

Had Tom's powers of perception been more sharp, he would have guessed that the athletic fellow in a bright warm up and running shoes heading toward him was in his early to mid 30's, but the bearded fellow was actually 40.

"Tom, I'm Jim Lifowitz. You were my idol in high school. I chased you in every race, about half a minute per mile behind. Have you got a few seconds? Let me show you something."

They walked past the patients' rooms to a little alcove away from the main area of the Heart Center. A hospital sign saying "Doctors Only" had been amended in scribble to say "Psych cases only."

The room they entered looked like it had originally been a storage room, but was turned into a customized office. The visible material on the walls was too much stimulation for Tom's state of mind. As Jim rummaged through a big file drawer looking for something, Tom's eyes made a tour of the high points around this avant garde office.

Over the door was a quote, "If exercise were a pill it would be the most heavily prescribed medicine—with a world record success rate." In the middle of the biggest wall was a picture of Ralph Paffenbarger, with the title, "our father." There were pictures people of all sizes and shapes, finishing marathons in Charlotte, New York, Washington, Atlanta, Chicago, and Honolulu, with inscriptions similar to the one from the CEO of one of the top 5 US corporations—"You made this possible—the greatest moment of my life." A famous rock star from the 60's was pictured, with band members, at the finish line of the San Francisco marathon, with the inscription "Finally, something positive to be addicted to!" A framed certificate with Jim Lifowitz's name on it, noted that he was the last finisher in the Disney Marathon. Next to it was a picture of his father and him finishing that marathon.

Over-stimulated and a bit confused by the collage of memories and the slow working of his mind at that time of night, Tom asked, "I read about Paffenbarger in one of my classes. Is he your father?"

Dr. Life wheeled around from his search in the old filing cabinet and his face lit up. "Oh, that would be a compliment, but no."

"Isn't he the epidemiologist for the US Department of Health who did the long-term studies showing a significant reduction in the incidence of heart disease among those who exercised, and the more exercise, the greater the reduction?"

"Yea," noted the doctor. For example, exercisers who burned only a moderate number of calories per week, reduced their chance of a fatal heart attack by about 25%—and a 50% reduction was achieved by those who burned more through exercise. Dr. Paffenbarger also showed that your chances of surviving a heart attack were significantly greater as the amount of exercise increased—that's probably what pulled your friend through—even the walking."

"Do you think that running is better."

The doctor's face reflected the seriousness of the subject. He responded with the passion of a professional who is trying to save the life of a client.

"There's no doubt in my mind. Of course, these days it's difficult to even get people to walk 5 minutes extra. I had the hospital reallocate a staff parking lot to our designated rehab lot, because it is further away. The 5-7 minutes of extra walking to our offices and extra 10 minutes to the rehab facility becomes significant exercise for some of our hopelessly sedentary patients. More recent research has shown that even that small amount of exercise will give most of my patients a significant protective effect. Running three times a week reduces your chance of heart problems about 80%."

Tom noticed for the first time that in a corner of the room a cassette player was appropriately playing Joan Baez singing his favorite song from the past: Dylan's "Forever Young."

Tom suddenly felt a kinship with the doctor, as if what had been a wall of eccentricity suddenly became an initiation ceremony. "I used to play that song as I drove to my most difficult workouts in highschool and college. There was something about his old songs—either by him or Baez—which got my mind right for the workout."

"It's interesting to me," said Dr. Life, "how some artists can get right through to you, I can't tell you why, but I get that feeling when I listen to some of the old Dylan songs."

"Why did you get into this field?" asked Tom.

"That guy got me to do it." smiled Jim, pointing to the picture of Paffenbarger on the wall. "I had to do a case study report in an epidemology course and ran across his research. Then I met him. He is a quiet, non-assuming guy, a true hero. Back in the 50's and early 60's, when nobody but Dr. Kenneth Cooper promoted that exercise had anything to do with health, Paffenbarger quietly cranked out this amazing research. Most medical leaders of that period thought that his work would only be interesting to students of medical history. They were convinced that everything could be eventually cured by drugs or surgery. Ralph quietly and patiently showed them that there is a powerful ancient healing device which could virtually wave a wand over the body and keep it healthy, and that is exercise."

"Oh. Here it is!" said the doctor as he pulled out a file of old pictures and opened it up. Tom was breaking the tape in a regional 2 mile cross country championship in high school, and in the background was a clean-shaven, crew cut version of Dr. Jim Lifowitz. "This was as close as I came to you in a race. Of course, I still had another loop of the field to do!"

"But tell me, do you really believe that running can help one avoid heart attacks better than, say, tennis, or golf?"

Lifowitz laughed. "Golf has the protective effect of a strenuous game of bridge, and tennis is not much better. It's a matter of our function, Tom. We were designed to run long distances. When we do it regularly, our cardiovascular system smiles and rewards us with more vitality; more years to our life and more life to our years."

"If you run a marathon every 6 months, and eat like a marathoner—you're not going to have a heart attack—unless you have some extremely unusual plumbing, or electrical connections. If we can get your friend Sam to do the Peachtree Road Race, we may save his life. I've had hundreds of patients who wouldn't start exercise when I told them to, but got swept up in the powerful wave of Peachtree. Many have gone on to do marathons, and the ones who have died, didn't die of heart disease."

Tom was still a bit confused. "Why do you think you have continued to run all these years? I've just endured too much pain."

An inspired look returned to Dr. Jim's face. "While it's easy for exercise to hurt—I went through years of that, myself—I've discovered that slowing down at the beginning of each workout is the key to the whole experience. When you slow down, the body rewards you in a hundred ways. Tens of thousands of little doses of endorphins give you an incredible sense of relaxation and pleasure." Dr. Life read the questioning look on Tom's face. "Yes, there are only a few other experiences in life which can give such honest pleasure, and satisfaction. Our bodies were designed for endurance exercise, and they thank us in many ways when we do it."

When a call came in for "Dr. Life" to check on another patient, he left, telling Tom to call him for a run sometime. Tom walked out of the hospital feeling good about Sam's prospects, and was reinforced by this unexpected connection from the past. Somehow the throught that "Dr. Life" really did want to take a run with him was energizing.

There were no low points on Tom's rollercoaster ride home.

23

Sunday, March 18, 11am. "Suzi, I hate these message machines. Anyway, Good News! Sam seems to have survived a heart attack. His doctor said that without the regular walking he has been doing—he probably wouldn't have made the trip to the hospital—he had a major blockage. The heart is functioning well and he can resume walking within a few weeks. Get this. He wants to do the Peachtree. He made me go down to the news stand and buy him a newspaper, and forced me to mail the entry in for him. You may want to give him a call, he'd appreciate it. This is your Peachtree conscience telling you to get your entry into the mailbox now. Peachtree will fill up this weekend—today! I'm really sleepy now and this tape is running out.."

Wednesday, March 22, 5 pm. "Sorry I missed you, Tom. I went by to see Sam at Peachtree Hospital and he was sleeping. They're going to let him go home tomorrow. Doesn't that seem early? I tried to get out and run/walk twice this week and need a support group—any ideas? You can call me at work—555-3311. Oh yea, I definitely entered the Peachtree thing on July 4th, I wouldn't miss a chance to show up my former friend in Boston. Of course, if this extra 20 pounds just wants to 'fall off', I'll let it."

Friday, March 24, 7am. "What are you doing Suzi, getting your day started so early—you must be out on a run—Ha. I talked to Sam and he would like to get some good walking shoes. There's only one place in Atlanta where they know shoes—how about meeting us at Phidippides in Ansley Mall at 11am tomorrow? See you there."

As Tom left his car in the Ansley Mall parking lot, a chemical reaction occurred, the smell of fresh bagels being absorbed by a hungry man. By the time he had interacted with the mid-morning bagel bunch and settled into the "breakfast bench" in front of Phidippides, Suzi pulled up and helped him sample the last 'cinnamon and raisin' in the bag, which was still warm.

Suzi was expecting Sam to arrive in a wheelchair, but he walked up to them looking as healthy as just about anyone in the store. "The doctor wants me to be active, and has actually encouraged me to walk in the Peachtree. He told me that studies of heart attack patients showed that those who had goals within the first 2 weeks of the attack recovered twice as fast as those who did not. He also said that those with exercise goals developed a much better attitude than the others. Tom, he also told me to tell you that he's been waiting for your call. That was the extent of his message to you."

"Oh," said Suzi. "I read an article on Dr. Lifowitz recently. He runs about 4 marathons each year and uses them as his vacation. He is such a believer in exercise that he was criticized by a very obese doctor who thought that drugs and surgery were the answer. The writer of the article said in a note made just as the magazine went to press the large critic had died of a heart attack. When they tried to reach Dr. Life for comment, he was out on a run!"

As they walked into the store, Suzi mentioned that she was ready to look at shoes, but not ready to buy. "I heard that this place has the best selection, but charges more for shoes than other stores in town."

This hit a nerve with Tom, whose most satisfying work experiences were individualizing shoes to the needs of a customer in a store with a similar philosophy. "My former female friend used to think that too," said Tom, "but when she called around—even to the discount stores—she found that some were a dollar lower, some the same, and that Phidippides had lower prices on many shoes. But even if the price here is a few dollars higher, you're saving money in the long run—getting advice which can avoid aches, pains, doctor bills, and a shoe that is not designed for your foot."

When Suzi asked how Phidippides differed from the other sport shoe stores, Tom explained that he had to re-learn about these differences, the hard way. Three years ago, after being away from the business for 10 years, he decided that

he still knew enough about shoes to pick his own, from a discount catalog. The first one was the wrong size, even though

---

The Top Five Reasons Why You Need Shoe Advice

1. Even the better running companies are using gimmicks in their design: Some of the gimmicks work, and some don't.

2. There's always a reason why the catalog offers a dramatic discount on a given shoe.

3. The same shoe may be made in different factories—making each significantly different in the way it fits, and in the many subtle ways it works when you run.

4. Only people who are really into running shoes can keep up with the gossip on running shoes—due to constant feedback they receive from hundreds of customers each week who really use the shoes for exercise.

5. Only experienced running staff people can look at you running in a shoe and tell whether it really fits—and works with your foot in the right way.

---

he had tried on the same model in a shoe store. On his second try, the shoe was made in a different factory—even a different country from the one that fit well in the store—and looked the same in the catalog. Because of the blisters it produced, he lost interest in running for several months. Finally, he bought the top-of-the-line shoe—$110 value for only $49—only to find that it was designed for a type of foot that he didn't have, forcing his foot into an injury.

"You mean," asked Suzi, "that the more

expensive shoes won't give you more insurance from injury?"

"In many cases, it is just the opposite," said Tom. "The higher the price, the more orthopedic devices are usually on the shoe. This means that if your foot is not in need of those devices, the cadillac shoe could actually *cause* injury."

Sam was ready to start, and Suzi became fascinated with the process. A woman in her mid 30's asked Sam what he had been doing for exercise, and how he expected to use the shoes. Then she asked him some specific questions about his feet, the success of past shoes, aches and pains, and other items. She was very articulate, pleasant, and very professional in her procedures.

Suzi took Tom aside and confided "This place has a neat feel to it. The staff people are knowledgeable and are helpful. I'm what you might call a 'power shopper' and haven't experienced this atmosphere in a long time."

Next, the staff person brought out 2 pairs of shoes and made Sam walk up and down the arcade outside the store. The Phidippidean noticed several things about Sam's feet which dictated changing to a different set of shoes. She explained how the extra support in the second batch would not only give better comfort for his specific needs, they would cut down on the potential of injury due to the way his foot rolled from side to side.

Suzi remembered how she had read a shoe review in a fitness magazine and purchased a shoe with that writer's advice. It seemed to cause some major

aches and pains in her ankle. When she confronted the woman who helped Sam, she learned that in some cases the magazine copy is taken from the write-up given by the shoe advertiser in the magazine. Even when a great expert gives state-of-the-art information, there are small oscillations in the foot which are not noticed until a trained foot observer sees the shoe and the foot walking or running down the pavement. Suzi was so pleased with the information she received about her foot and her ankle problem, that she decided to get a good pair, also. Tom admitted that he had just learned something new, that some of his past injuries may have been encouraged by his failure to keep up with some of the new shoe technology inside the shoe. He decided to just see what a recommended shoe would feel like. Two of the suggested models fit like a glove, and made him feel like an athlete again. "This shoe gives me back the bounce that was in my legs 10 years ago."

The manager of the store, in her 40's, warned Tom with a smile, not to count on that for every run.

"It's like so many products today," said Sam, "technical products are becoming very specialized. The right one becomes an extension of your foot, actually improving the operation. The wrong one becomes, at best, an aggravation, and at worst a big bill at the doctor's office.

"The best advice is to get the best advice," said Tom. I know, because I've got a closet full of bargains to prove it!"

THE DIFFERENCE BETWEEN A DREAM...AND A VISION

26

Hearing some one coming to his front door, Tom raised up to sitting position from his favorite, aerobic basketball-watching position. Realizing it was Suzi, he told her to come in.

"I'm here to pick you up."

"But I don't have time today, Suzi. Everything is running longer than I thought. You and Sam can go on without me."

As he watched Suzi size up the basketball game on the TV, the chips and dip on the table next to the couch and the drinks in the cooler underneath the couch, Tom knew he was in trouble.

"What's the real issue, Tom? You aren't motivated, are you? You're the weak link in our group. Sam must exercise for survival. I made a vow to show a friend that he was wrong, that I could stick to a program and reach an exercise goal. But you, you're above all of this."

Sometimes guilt works. Tom reluctantly got up, followed Suzi's step-by-step instructions (including turning the TV off and grabbing two photos of himself) and walked to the car. Under the strain of Suzi's applied pressure, Tom admitted that he wanted to watch the North

Carolina game of the NCAA "final four" tournament. He also stated "for the record," that he was doing this because Suzi asked him, and "not in the best of spirits." Sam agreed that it was hard for him to give up the two hours he had looked forward to, camped in front of his TV set, but Dr. Life had given him marching orders.

"You owe me one," said Tom.

"No, YOU will owe me one—just wait," insisted Suzi. Besides, you'll like the guy who conducts the seminar.

"OK, I'll admit two things. First, I don't want to give up good basketball time to listen to some motivational, 'you can do anything' type session. And yes, I'm having trouble with my exercise motivation because for me, it doesn't compute."

"You mean you can't identify with us, Sam and I."

"It's more complex than that. I'm motivated by your excitement, and energy. But I have some mental scars from the intense training in my past. For 15 years my exercise was directed toward a specific goal, with specific challenges and specific rewards. There were few other things in my life. My single,

Exerpts from <u>The Five Stages of a Runner</u> {see Galloway's Book on Running, pp24-31}

Stage 1: Beginner

"...precarious...a struggle within and without...running threatening to less active friends...groups very motivational...many beginners stop and start again 10-15 times before they get the habit established. As you make progress you find within yourself the strength and security to keep going. At first you're "just visiting" that special world when you go out for a run. But gradually you begin to change. You get used to the positive relaxed feeling. Your body starts cleaning itself up, establishing muscle tone, circulating blood and oxygen more vigorously. One day you find you're addicted and the beginner becomes a jogger."

Stage 2: Jogger

"...secure with running...hard to start...but...can identify with those who are addicted...rarely a plan or goal...a bit more independent...races as motivational stepping stones...set back to beginner by layoff caused by injury, bad weather, partner dropping out. By piecing together a growing series of successful and non-threatening experiences, you begin the transition into a more fit lifestyle."

Stage 3: Competitor

"...not all enter this stage...competitive streak hidden in all of us...can be a great motivator...problem when it becomes the goal...plan your running around races...always new training techniques and competitor tries them all—later to learn many are contradictory...missing a run seems to spell racing doom...making workouts into races...pushing too far and getting injured...Strengths we have never used lie buried in each of us. Being challenged to our limits through competition helps these surface."

Stage 4: Athlete

"...more meaning in the drive to fulfill your potential...a state of mind not bound by age, performance or place in the running pack...victory lies in the quality of effort...internalize competition and transcend it...continuous re-evaluation...planning...Great athletes at any level realize that 'success is in the eye of the per-former'. There can be success in every experi-ence. If you can seize upon the positive aspect of each experience you can string together a series of successes that form a pattern of progress.

Stage 5: Runner

"...blends the best elements of all previous stages...the runner is a happy person...primary focus in life is not running, but you get so much satisfaction from the experience itself that running has become a necessary and stable part of your active lifestyle...enjoying peace and inner reflection of the solitary run more than in earlier stages...As a runner...you appreciate the creative and positive aspects of each and let them enrich your running life."

focused dream didn't happen. I've dealt with the failure issues, but other aspects of my life have filled in the time and focus energy which I used in my goal pursuit."

"Years ago, in one of our workout groups," continued Tom, "we hatched a theory which could explain all of my problems. The concept was that running fast killed brain cells. The longer you ran fast during a workout, the more cells destroyed. If that were true I have ample reason for the days when I feel lethargic and can't think clearly. Over the years, I ran hundreds of workouts. There just aren't many thinking cells left."

Suzi had another theory. As they drove to the session she told them about the "Five Stages of a Runner" she had heard about at the fitness vacation. It sounded to her as if Tom had gotten up to the 4th stage—but never gained the satisfaction of that level—or the consolidation of the running experience in the 5th stage. Tom's reply was "that sounded like a shrink talking," and "I don't believe in 'stages' anyway."

Suzi explained that this session was designed to help one put a lifestyle change program into a more meaningful context. The speaker was doing this—in his spare time—as a special request to Suzi, and a few other professionals.

When Sam asked how well this concept had worked, Suzi said that for those who were ready to take responsibility for their health and well-being, it was extremely empowering.

As they entered the house of the leader—where the session was to be given—Sam noted how comfortable it felt. There were clothes draped over pieces of furniture, and kids' stuff lying around. The others were already sitting on the floor in the living room, chatting and laughing about failed attempts at lifestyle changes. One woman, who had unsuccessfully tried to immerse herself into the macrobiotic diet, was offering for sale a 50 pound sack of brown rice at a bargain price. Others tried, humorously, to palm off pyramid hats, crystals, thigh creams, and other miracle change devices.

The leader briefly introduced them to the concept of lifestyle mental rehearsal, with a few stories about his failures. Among them, his first wife who was so frustrated with his plan to help her lose weight that she showed him—she gained 100 pounds in one year. "I must admit that this put some terminal strains on our relationship."

While they moved into the family room, where the furniture had been moved against the walls, Sam told Suzi that he liked the leader's sense of humor, and the cheers from the audience when he admitted that his approach was not founded or backed up by research. After a few basic instructions, he got started.

A Vision—or a Dream?

"Lets talk about the difference between a dream and a vision, for starters. Oh yea, you need to know that I'm not defensive about my ideas here, it's only what I believe in and base my whole life upon. Seriously, after my experience in my first marriage, I've learned to separate my ego from my advice. I welcome you to take it or leave it. I love questions, but I will not argue. First let's talk about dreams. These are the things that you may (or may not) remember having at night. Just reserve the sleeping period for your dreams. They have no effect on behavior. Dreams may have a facade of reality, with an underlying structure of fantasy. Dreams do not effect behavior to any lasting extent.

On the other hand, visions give you a glimpse of what you can accomplish, and allow you to fill in the behavioral components which can bring it to reality. When you have a realistic concept of what you can accomplish, a plan of action in several component categories, and an image of what you want to do at a certain point in time, you're got the makings of a vision which can change some significant behavior patterns in your life.

You can *dream* that you're going to find that miracle diet which will leave you slim and vigorous. In contrast, a *vision* of yourself in 5 years will include a realistic view of yourself, the diet you will be eating, exercise which you enjoy doing, how you will be feeling about yourself, etc. In a dream you do away with all of the problems, but in a vision, you deal with them, overcome them through a plan of specific activities. You teach yourself to feel good about yourself, and develop a specific plan of action which will tend to maintain this positive image.

Belief Exercise

"I believe in my ability to make the changes."

"I know that there will be struggles and I believe in my ability to get through them."

"I believe in my creative capacity to find fun in the experience."

"By believing that I will make these positive changes, I am making many intuitive changes occur inside me—which will allow the changes to occur more effectively and more efficiently."

"These changes in my life are happening and are becoming a solid part of my belief environment."

"By immersing myself into the belief framework, I am connecting up to a greater, positive force."

"Nothing can mess with my belief environment."

Your Own Belief Environment

While visions can be very powerful, they're not enough to actually make the changes. You must not only believe in the vision, you need to have a belief environment—a framework or structure which can handle stress during the process—and reinforce you through your system of achievement. Through your overall vision, you can mold your belief in your ability to make changes, and the benefits of the changes themselves.

I am convinced that we are all capable of constructing a belief environment. It's basic to each of us, even though we may choose not to use it. Through more than a hundred thousand generations, we, as human organisms, have developed very complex internal ways of dealing with beliefs of all types. It's not enough to say you believe—you must connect with the structure inside which can deal with lapses of commitment, challenges to components of your vision—and even greater challenges to the vision itself. You're going to get those challenges, you know that. You can use the process to pull together the parts of your psyche which tell you to push through doubt, discomfort, and insecurity. It's there, but each of us has to learn how to reach for it, build it, and fill in the many areas which surround and form the framework. We strengthen each of those components when we regularly challenge ourselves in a meaningful way. I know that many of you are using the Peachtree Road Race to stimulate such a challenge.

Now you don't have to call it 'belief

environment'. Some of the nicknames given are belief mountain, tower, freight train, etc. Find a term which means something to you, and make it a part of you.

It's not enough to have an image of what you want to look like, what you need to eat, how you need to exercise, etc. You must know why you want to look that way, eat that way and exercise that way. You must absorb every part of your vision into your belief environment, and inhabit it, live it, wear it.

Now don't expect to do all of this immediately. That's what the following exercises are all about. To a certain extent you can energize, mold and construct your belief environment as

you go through your program. At the very least, you must commit yourself to set up the foundation, with a commitment to expand it.

Relaxation

"It helps us all to relax before we get too involved into the visions. I don't believe in an extensive relaxation exercise—because many people go to sleep during the process—and I have to start all over. Too much of a good thing. We'll do a shortened version which I call a 'mental eraser'.

I know that many of you experience anxiety and stress when you approach some of the behavioral aspects of your program, especially exercise. The

---

The Mental Eraser

1. It helps to have some exotic, relaxing music—which gets you into a relaxed state of mind and doesn't bring to consciousness any specific images.

2. Lie down on the floor, or a soft pad of some type. Get totally comfortable—you don't want to experience any discomfort in any specific area of your body. You want to feel comfortable in the reclining position—on your back. If you have to prop yourself up with pillows or towels—do it.

3. Breathe in through your mouth and out through your nose. Every 3rd or 4th breath, exhale completely, and then inhale completely. Stay very relaxed and try to breathe using your diaphram, with the stomach rising and falling more than the chest.

4. Think of nothing. A good mental image is that of a mental eraser working its way quickly through your brain, eliminating tension and stress, or mental activity from any area of your life at this moment—and only this moment.

5. At first, concentrate on the sound and experience of breathing. Gradually let your mind and body just exist, in a thoughtless, tensionless, and comfortable state.

6. After about 4-5 minutes in this state, you're ready to move on to your next activity. Gently and slowly start your visual exercises.

'mental eraser' can knock the edge off much of this.

They spread out on the floor so that no one touched another. The leader began by saying that due to the pressures, stresses, and over-stimulation of modern life, he has had more success in "getting into" the mental rehearsal when we start with a mental erasing first. It was not mandatory, however.

Body Shape

"Now let's get right into the technique by visualizing what you're going to look like in 5 years." Close your eyes, clean out all thoughts from your brain. Now get a vision, a realistic image of yourself 5 years from now. For some of you there will be a few more wrinkles, and a few more grey hairs. For some men, there will be less covering on the head. But lets get to the real point here. Think of those places on your body which have too much fat deposited, your "fat pads." Go from the top of your shoulders to the bottom of you legs systematically reducing each area of your body which has extra layers. Don't put too much pressure on yourself by erasing all of it, just make a reduction. When you get to the thighs and hips, visualize enough of the fat removed so that you can see better muscle definition. Now if you're really brave, lets work on the stomach; actually, you'll be amazed at how close you'll come to your realistic vision. Get a clear image of a flat stomach which looks the way you'd like it to look. You have a license to be optimistic, but please be realistically optimistic.

After going through the body—section

by section—back off and see what you look like 5 years from now. If you need to make a few more changes in specific areas, do that now. Look at yourself. You are proud of the changes you have made in 5 years.

Next, get an image of what you'll look like 4 years from now. Go through the same process from head to toe, realizing that the result won't be quite as significant as that seen in 5 years.

Now pull up the image of yourself 3 years from now. Each stage is only slightly different from the next one. Be realistic, now!

Two years from now, what will you look like? Focus on that. This image is not too different from what you look like now.

The next image is that of yourself next year. In one year you will have made a significant start in this process. As you look at each part that needs to be changed can you notice much difference? Not too much. The first year sets up the changes inside, which are often not noticed on the outside for months. That's OK.

Finally, go back to our original vision, 5 years from now, a realistic but slimmer and more athletic body. Lets go over the places that were former fat pads, which you have molded and changed. You've done it, and you're very proud of the discipline you've developed, and the positive lifestyle habits you've incorporated as a natural part of your life. Give yourself a hand!

The next 12 months are the toughest of

the 5 year plan, because you're changing direction. Whenever you shift away from old habits, you'll develop some significant internal resistance.

They took a "vision break" to look at pictures of body types, and trace some shapes of themselves, from the pictures they brought, showing the progress they will make in the next 5 years.

The Food Vision

To get to your 5 year shape plan, your selective choice of food will help in two ways. By avoiding foods with fat and concentrated sugar, you'll avoid putting fat on. But as you shift to some high performance, complex carbohydrate foods, you'll find the energy you need to burn off the blanket on your body. This isn't a nutrition session, so you'll need to set up the nutritional program which works best for you. Talk to a good 'food doctor'.

OK—you power-eaters—close your eyes and focus on the foods you now eat, which are counter productive to your body vision goal. If you really like some of these foods, you'll want to always feel that they are available.

Lets get a vision of your diet 5 years from now. It is filled with good-tasting, low fat foods, which give energy. The decadent foods that you really like, such as donuts or ice cream, are still in your diet, but they are eaten only occasionally and in small doses. You get the same satisfaction out of eating half a donut, once a week, as you do now when you eat 2 donuts every other day.

You have added a number of new foods to your diet in the form of low fat snacks, which keep you energized all day. During the first year of the program, there were some foods which you knew would help you, but didn't taste good. Through lots of sampling you've learned to like many of these foods, and now, 5 years later, you eat some of the low-fat snacks several times a day.

You've changed your dietary pattern so that you eat all day long. You're enjoying healthy snacks every hour or so, in small amounts, infusing energy in your body before you get hungry or feel a let-down. As you enjoy the new foods, you feel the energy infusion which burns a bit more away from the 'fat blanket' you want to reduce. You're proud of yourself for eating regularly, instead of over-eating in a few large meals.

Your diet four years from now will have a bit more of the negative foods, than your first year diet, and not as many of the new snacks. But you've made most of the innovations.

Three years from this date you are starting to gain control over the decadent foods. You're still eating them regularly, but the high fiber-energy snacks are becoming more interesting because you find that they work, giving you sustained energy. The innovations in lower fat recipes and food choices are challenging you to test new items.

Your food program in two years is only starting to change in substance. You've made some significant substitutions in foods, however, which have lowered the number of mid-morning or mid-afternoon "lulls" when you lack energy and concentration.

When you look at your diet one year from now, you'll see very little change from today. You're beginning to shift to alternative foods which lower the fat. The big shift is that you've realized that you're headed toward a very different diet, and you not only know that you will enjoy it, but you will appreciate the taste of some of the lower fat choices.

Go back to the vision of your diet 5 years from now. You've made the changes and like the foods. While you've not given up the decadent items, you don't have much craving for them any more. You've done it. Give yourselves a hand.

You can use all types of visualizations to tie into your ultimate food vision. As you eat the high fiber-energy snacks, visualize pumping your muscles with energy while you starve the fat cells in your fat pads. These images get very complex, and help to tie the whole program together.

They took a break and looked at menus of successful diet changers, at 1, 2, 3, 4 and 5 year intervals. Other interesting items were available for copying: recipes, samples of complex carbo snacks, etc. This was a fun break, because several of the participants brought low fat covered dishes for sharing.

During the break, Suzi told Sam and Tom quietly that she was astounded that neither had said anything about the presentation. Sam said that it made sense to him, and opened his mind to other possible goals, reinforcements. He had great doubts that he would spend the time to actually do the mental exercises.

"But that's why he's doing this," whispered Tom, "he's looking for new clients." Suzi countered with the fact that most of his sessions are full—and that's why he's doing some free programs like this—and then pinned Tom down by asking him how he actually felt.

"You have to realize that I'm really sceptical about this type of stuff. It seems to be mostly fluff and requires so much follow-up, as Sam recognized. The principles are sound, world-class athletes have used a variation of this, instinctively, for decades. On the positive side, he has done a better job of connecting the components together into the 'big picture'. This is an interesting combination of "I believe" and 'Here's How'.

Just as they were called back into the session, Suzi whispered to Tom, "So you're going to give him a break."

The Vision of Exercise

"For lifestyle change, nothing helps pull everything together like exercise. More than anything, it is a performance statement to the whole organism that you are doing something positive toward your goal. It helps to mentally talk yourself through this several times every day. Positive reinforcement—even verbally—is very powerful over time.

Your exercise is the machinery which drives the change, and the furnace which burns up the excess fuel. Most dieters realize this if and when they lose the targeted weight, the design, colors and lines of the chassis look great, and they've found the fuel that will keep deposits from accumulating. But without an engine you really shouldn't take it out on the expressway, you really shouldn't.

- Because you're exercising, you have the power to shape your body up the way you want.

- Dieting alone will just take off the blanket—it's gonna leave the same sags—in the same places. To get some form and function, which is attractive, you must exercise.

- Exercise doesn't have to hurt to give all the benefits.

Everyone has a preferred exercise, one that at the very least is not intimidating, and at best gives satisfaction and pleasure. To burn fat, you must be able to keep moving—to 'rev' up the engine and keep it cranking—over an extended period of time. So you want to choose exercises like walking, cycling, cross country ski machines, rowing, running, etc., which can allow you to do this. Exercises which force you to stop and start will only help a little. The continuous ones develop the furnace.

A question came in from the audience. "Which are the most efficient fat burners?"

"Generally the pecking order is as follows:
1. Running
2. Cross Country Skiing machines
3. Rowing
4. Cycling
5. Walking

But don't even think about that now. Your job is to just find one you can do easily, and one that you can keep doing comfortably, for an extended period. Once you get hooked on the experience of exercise you can shift to a stronger 'brand,' if you wish.

I want you to close your eyes now and get very quiet. Five years from now you will be exercising 3-4 times per week, and enjoying it. Get an image of yourself doing this. You may occasionally push yourself a little on some of the sessions, but most are just enjoyable, and give you more pleasure than you could ever imagine. One of the reasons is that you are starting each session slowly and have found how to steer your exercise so that each one is a success.

One of the greatest breakthroughs is the realization that YOU determine how you feel afterwards. YOU can make each session feel good.

Five years from now, you're not concerned about how many calories you're burning, what you're wearing or anything else. You're hooked. The experience is a reward in itself.

You've adjusted your diet so that you eat an energizing snack before exercise which gives sustained energy—and you've naturally learned to avoid the foods which cause you to be sluggish—mostly those with fat and high sugar content.

As you exercise, you pull up an image of burning off the 'pad' in the areas you want burned. And you also visualize the building of muscles where you want them built. You don't need to see immediate results, you're working on your next 5 year plan.

Four years from now you've made most of those visualization changes in your exercise. You may not be completely hooked, for there are some days when it's harder to get out there.

About three years from this date you will have learned to enjoy exercise every session. There will still be days when you don't want to get out there—but you find the motivation to do so—and feel great afterward.

Two years from now you feel the changes in your positive attitude about exercise taking hold, but you go up and down on some days. You've worked out most of the mistakes, starting too hard, trying to keep up with someone else who is in better condition, etc.

By this time next year you will have established a habit of exercise. While you had some lapses, you made it out there most days and got it in. On most of those sessions you felt so good afterward that you reinforced yourself. You know from the strength of your belief environ-ment that you will continue to improve both motivation, and conditioning.

Now we're going to put it all together. Five years from now, you have become a healthy animal that craves exercise, enjoys it naturally and yet is not obsessive when a day has to be missed. The exercise gives you a boost which lasts all day. Your diet is filled with good tasting snacks all day long, which keep you energized and up-beat. You're proud of the fact that you've learned to like foods which are low in fat, yet keep you energized throughout the day. The exercise and the diet have given you a good attitude which has positively affected your work and personal relationships.

As you look in the mirror, you realize that you are continuing to be a success, and that you have a positive key to your future. Congratulations and give yourselves a hand!

As the session ended and participants began their conversational chatter, Suzi told Tom that he looked unusually pensive.

Tom thought for a few moments and said, "I can see that a primary reason why I never achieved at the level which I could have is I had a dream instead of a vision."

CRUISIN'

No one wanted to talk about the session, as the three amigos drove back to Tom's house, so Sam and Tom discussed the NCAA "Final Four" tournament. Both were instantly energized by the news from the oldies station that UNC had won their quarter-final game, and would move on the the NCAA mens' basketball finals in Seattle.

Suzi had had enough of the basketball talk by the time they arrived at Tom's house, and wanted to take a walk on the beautiful Spring day. Sam and Tom agreed to take a tour of the neighborhood with her, as she talked about the exercise called "CRUISIN" which she had started.

"After three weeks of 'just walking', said Suzi, "I was ready to move on, to add some pizazz. I'm not saying that the walking was getting boring, not totally. But after the walk, on some days, I started to feel like I hadn't done very much of a workout."

She explained how several of the folks at the summer fitness vacation used this method to get started, and two of them still used it as their primary form of exercise. While some walkers become

'cruisers' to get more quality and fat-burning out of their exercise, runners who are getting back after a long lay-off are also using it to minimize tiredness and risk of injury.

After about 3 minutes of walking, Suzi jogged for 60 seconds, then skipped for 10-15 seconds, before settling back into a comfortable walk. Tom and Sam kept up with her on the jog, but walked through the skipping. Suzi explained how this gave her a much more invigorating experience.

"It also burns more fat," noted Tom. "Not that you need to lose any off your dainty body."

"Speak for yourself, Tiny Tom," said Suzi, and she took off walking and jogging up a 60-80 yd hill.

Sam had lagged behind, so the other 2 walked back and apologized for getting carried away.

"You two go ahead," said Sam. "I've got my heart rate monitor and know exactly what I need to do, but if you want to stay back with the 'slow polk' long enough to answer a question. What was that statement about more fat-burning, Tom?"

Cruisin'

Why:

For those who want a bit more challenge than that presented by walking alone, the infusion of more vigorous activity increases the fat-burning, and condenses the time needed to get a good workout.

What:

A method of alternating vigorous activity—with less vigorous activity. By changing the use of muscle groups, at different effort levels, one can cover longer distances—the factor which burns more fat, producing a better stress release, and a more powerful attitude boost.

Example:

A beginner would walk slowly for 2-4 minutes, and walk faster for 30-60 seconds. For someone with a good background of walking, or other endurance exercise: 2-3 minutes of comfortable walking would be followed by 1 minute of slow jogging.

Other options:

The inserts to comfortable walking can be any other activity which tends to speed up the metabolism—skipping, jumping, race-walking, etc. Make sure that the inserts are not traumatic and that the new movements and exertions are gradually introduced to the muscles.

A workout plan:

Three times a week, set aside 30 minutes. When you've settled into a comfortable walking pace, gradually increase the duration to 45-60min, or start the inserts. Be conservative at first, walking for 4-5 minutes and jogging (etc) for 30-60 seconds. After a week or two, if you want to increase the exertion level of your exercise session, you may decrease the walking time between jogs, increase the length of the jogs, or increase the total time of the session. It is better not to settle into a set pattern—but keep the variety. That will allow you to have more control over the fun you're having—and make each session unique. Make sure that you don't increase the overall intensity or duration more than about 10% when you're making an increase.

Primary Benefits:

In contrast to running continuously, walking-break sessions allow you to go farther with less pounding and less damage. This means that you'll burn more calories

When do you phase out the walking breaks?

You never need to phase them out. Even experienced marathoners benefit from them on all long runs—particularly those that are over 15 miles in length. When the long runs get significantly longer than the daily ones, you may gradually cut out some or all of the breaks on the shorter runs. Again—you don't have to ever cut them out—even if you've shifted to mostly running.

To maximize fat-burning, gradually increase the sessions beyond 45 minutes.

Jogging Breaks Increase Fat Burning

@50 calories/mi	Total walk:
@55 calories/mi	Jog inserts every 4-5 min
@60 calories/mi	Jog inserts every 3-4 min
@65 calories/mi	Jog inserts every 2 min
@70 calories/mi	Jog inserts every 1 min
@75 calories/mi	Race Walking:
@80 calories/mi	Jogging for 2 minutes, walking 1min
@85 calories/mi	Jogging for 3 minutes, walking 1 min
@90 calories/mi	Jogging for 4 minutes, walking 1 min
@95 calories/mi	Jogging for 5-8 minutes, walking 1 min
@100 calories/mi	Running continuously

March Exercise Routine

Sam:
30 minutes of slow walking
4 times a week
at the rehab clinic

Suzi:
30 minutes of slow walking
3 times a week
to and from the office
(parking 15 min walk away)

Tom:
- A one-hour basketball game
  once a week after work,
  'old farts' vs 'upstarts'
- 30 minutes of running
  twice a week after work—
- A long one which increased to 60 minutes
  by Apr.

"Walking burns about 50 calories per mile. Running burns about 100 per mile. By infusing your walks with some sections of running—or at least some increased activity—you get the engines 'revved-up' to burn more calories per mile."

"But what I noticed most," said Suzi, "is that on the sessions with jogging—I feel so much better—invigorated, and glowing. It seems to relieve more stress and leave me mentally refreshed."

After their 45 minute "cruise" around the neighborhood, Tom was in a particularly good mood, and Suzi took advantage of this, asking: "How does it feel to be a 'slow poke'?"

"I finished my first one-hour run yesterday," reported Tom, "and was feeling it this morning. This crusin' allows me to get the legs moving, without pounding. They actually feel better now than they have all day."

* For additional information on getting started, see GALLOWAY'S BOOK ON RUNNING pp 32-36.

39

....

"So you're not going to join us, Suzi, because it's raining a little?"

"I don't know, Tom, it may be Spring fever or something—but I was thinking about backing up a little—and working on my 'belief environment'."

"I don't like the sound of this, Suzi, you commissioned me to be the enforcer, to keep you moving toward your Peachtree program on July 4th. I'm going to step in here, now. What's your problem, anyway?"

"No—I just thought that...I've been working, this week, on the diet portion of my 'belief environment', and was thinking that I could start this great new diet to lose weight, and exercise will be much easier."

"Tell us about it. Meet at the Park Street entrance to Piedmont Park."

"Well...OK...I Guess."

As they entered the park, walking 3 minutes and jogging 1 minute, the rain stopped, giving the impression that it might be clearing up. Sam mentioned how beautiful the reflection was: of the blue sky with grey clouds and the mid-

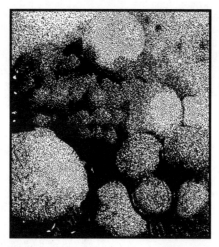

town skyline. Suzi complained that she had little energy to exercise since she went on the diet, which bothered Tom.

The Starvation Reflex

"You know that diets don't work Suzi. Besides, you're playing with a powerful, biological counter-attack."

"The Starvation Reflex," noted Suzi. "Yes, I heard about it during Galloway's fitness vacation. But I want to get rid of some of this baggage so I'll feel better when I get out there to exercise. I know that I'll look better. Besides, I read this article..."

They went back and forth. Tom told her about his experience in working with weight loss programs which he set up for various companies. Only about 20% of the enrollees stayed with the diet program, and almost all gained the weight back after a year, and then some.

"I feel like a used car salesman setting up these programs. There's a big market out there, and the diets will take off the pounds, but I'm really concerned about the after-effects. My boss tells me, all the time, to tone down my criticism of diets—because they compose a major segment of our income—but I suspect

The Starvation Reflex

Our ancient ancestors had to do without food for extended periods of time. In order to better survive, a series of very complex biological and psychological mechanisms inside us are set off when we deprive ourselves of food. Both the appetite and the accumulation of body fat is increased, in order to cope with the threat of starvation: The human organism can do without foods which we need and love to eat for an extended period of time, but is programmed to overcompensate. When the period of deprivation is over, the individual will gradually eat more calories than needed over another extended period of time, to store up more fat than before. This mechanism helped our ancient ancestors prepare for the next starvation period. If we've deprived ourselves of special (and often decadent) foods, we will tend to over-consume those foods at some time in the future, when they become available again.

1. The longer we wait between meals, the more we stimulate the fat-depositing enzymes, so that more of the next meal will be deposited as fat.

2. The longer we wait between meals, the more we stimulate our appetite, so that we will tend to over-eat, and accumulate more excess calories for fat storage.

3. Many people have a tendency to eat more decadent, fatty foods when they have been waiting a long time to eat, and the higher quantity of fat in these foods produces a greater deposition of body fat.

The longer we deprive ourselves of food, the more we are likely to trigger the starvation reflex. The body organism is stimulated to over-react to adversity, and over-deposit fat for the next deprivation period. Unfortunately, we are also programmed to over-consume food (especially items we really like—but try to avoid) when it is abundant (avoid buffet dinners).

Psychological Starvation

It is also counterproductive to tell ourselves that we will NEVER eat a given food again. While we all can deprive ourselves of our decadent favorites by following this over-strict rule, we're already setting up a powerful negative psychological mechanism. At some point, our appetite will build and when the forbidden food is available, we will almost certainly over-consume it.

It is always better to tell yourself that you will always have that food available, and that you will always be able to eat it. The secret is to physically and mentally (over a period of time) alter your expectations, your appetite, and your behavior toward the food, so that you'll learn to enjoy a small amount of it as much as you currently enjoy a larger amount.

that most, without exercise, are un-healthy.

As they started up a hill toward 14th Street, Tom noticed that Sam was trying to say something but was huffing and puffing. Tom slowed the pace by walking 4 minutes and jogging 30-45 seconds. Sam recovered and made his statement:

"I hate to interrupt the beginning of a beautiful argument," he said, "but I haven't heard of Galloway's starvation reflex."

"The worst part," noted Tom, "is that during a starvation program, the dieter doesn't want to exercise, and really doesn't have the energy or motivation to do anything physical. Without the muscle power to keep the fat burned off, a starvation diet survivor is biologically programmed to deposit more fat after the diet—without the "musclepower" to burn it off—so even more is stored during the "rebound" process.

"How do YOU know all of this," asked Suzi.

"I dated a nutritionist." The finality of his statement told everyone that the relationship was over. To get out of the awkward silence, Tom put the train of thought onto Sam's track. "Sam, you study ancient man. How does this compute in your field?"

"It matches up very well indeed. The early developers of the bodies we inherited didn't have the strength, the speed or the intelligence to compete with other animals for food. We evolved for millions of years by roaming long distances, gathering the leftovers of nature's dinner table. So we were designed to perform hours of extended, aerobic, movement—just to survive— every day. Periods of starvation and deprivation were common, and could have set up the biological responses you mention."

The physio/psycho development of early man was Sam's great life project. He had

---

A Dietary Plan for Peachtree Hunter/Gatherers *(especially those who want to lower the fat blanket)*

1. Eat small amounts of food all day. Instead of waiting 4-6 hours between meals, eat small, low fat, low sugar snacks continuously throughout the day. Bites of a high-soluable-fiber PowerBar every hour(one quarter to one half a bar), for example, will keep you energized and avoid the mid morning or mid afternoon "letdowns". **If you do this all day, day after day, you're teaching your body that it doesn't have to accumulate fat—that food is consistently available.**

2. You must eat enough food to keep from getting hungry. It's not enough to eat a carrot every hour, for example. You'll get extremely hungry and over-eat later.

3. Even if they don't taste great at first, you can teach yourself to enjoy low-fat, energy foods, which are not too concentrated with sugar. Keep eating a variety of these foods, in small amounts, over a long period of time, to develop a "taste" for them.

Foods to avoid:

1. Generally, all foods that have more than 15% of the calories in fat, unless you mix them. A pasta sauce in which 25% of the calories are in fat can be mixed sparingly with pasta (5% fat calories) for a delicious meal with only 10-12% fat calories. Of course, it is still better to use pasta sauce which has no fat.

2. Foods with high concentrations of sugar: soft drinks, fruit drinks, most fruits, and any foods which have lots of sugar without soluable fiber (it coats the lining of the stomach and slows down the release of the sugars).

3. Beware of the fatty add-ons. Baked Potatoes are great food, but adding just one tablespoon of sour cream will put fat on your body. Here is a list of common offenders: pizza, pasta with cream sauce, Salmon and other high fat fish, all fried foods, ramen noodles, popcorn with oil or butter. Salads are very healthy, but regular and "low fat" salad dressings make them high fat . For seasonings, try no-fat dressings, no-fat sour cream, salsa, low-fat soups, etc.

great stories and theories about the development of the long and winding human digestive tract, and how it extracted nutrients. Even some questionably nutritious weeds could keep our ancestors going.

Sam enjoyed describing the great periods of famine which most primitive peoples experienced regularly. "It is a natural human instinct to over-eat at a buffet, for example. When food is plentiful, we—as human animals—are programmed to over-eat. Body fat was an asset—a real functional hedge against the future famine which was certain to occur—for the first few million years of our existence.

"There is some evidence," said Sam, "that humans were most creative and most productive when they were in a hunter-gatherer mode. They ate small snacks found along the way for energy. The exercise and the regular carbohydrate snacks may have been the physiological connection which kept them energized. I believe that under these conditions the mind was more receptive to learning—and better able to respond to the challenges—which were abundant.

"Did your nutritionist friend change your diet?" Suzi asked Tom.

Tom had physically tightened up when this relationship was brought up before. "Her name is Susan—by the way—and she only tried by example, I guess. When I said I was going to stop eating ice cream, she told me I wouldn't. To prove to her wrong, I didn't bring any ice cream into the house for over a year, and

I didn't eat any at all. Meanwhile, she would eat her bowl of my favorite flavor—Breyers Chocolate Chip Mint—about once a week. Always in moderation, she was. One day I went over to a friend's house to help celebrate her daughter's birthday. Feeling that I was "above" my former addiction to the delicious substance, I took just one bite of the ice cream, then another, and in a short period of time I had eaten a half gallon. I couldn't believe it. She was right, I was back on the habit, eating it just about every night. I hated her for this—when *I* was to blame for being so stubborn—and encouraging the feast after the famine."

"Now that is a complex example of the starvation reflex," said Sam. "Tom, you deprived yourself of something which you dearly loved. This depravation probably set up the over-consumption in your future behavior."

"My last diet ended in a similar pattern," admitted Suzi. "I slimmed down for my 10th college reunion last year by trying one of those strict diets—yes, a starvation program. Boy did it take off the weight. I looked great when I saw my college friends. For a month or so, I felt great, and ate conservatively, then it hit. Like a great wave coming back to the shore, I absorbed all the food I could touch, and more, after each meal. It's finally stablized, I think, but I gained back all I had lost, and 20 pounds more."

"I wonder how you can change your eating habits, without the starvation problem," asked Suzi.

"Why don't you bring that question to the nutrition clinic at Phidippides, which Tom mentioned," said Sam. "I'm looking forward to it."

As Suzi started to sweat, a strange gutteral feeling of confidence came over her. Normally she would have pondered the next question over and over, and not asked it at all, but it just rolled out naturally. "What happened between you and her?"

"She...it was a lot of things." Tom started to hold back, but was also experiencing the relaxation and mutual confidence felt in an exercise group. "I guess I've never admitted it, but I wasn't ready for the growth process. I was secure in eating and living in such a way—and I couldn't deal with the thought that her suggestions were correct—it threatened me. She even considered the diet plans I implemented for my company to be unhealthy. I got into these gut-wrenching arguments with her because I reacted to my job being threatened. Now I argue with my boss because I believe that she was right, but I was pretty stubborn back then. In the end, I found it hard to date 'my conscience'."

"But you were right also," noted Suzi. "So many of the health problems are aggravated by obesity, especially the big killers of heart disease, diabetes and many forms of cancer. You helped people lose weight, lower their obesity, and lower their risk, right?"

"My boss keeps telling me that. Unfortunately, an increasing number of studies have shown—even on our program— that almost all of those who lost fat in

the program gained back more fat 3-5 years later. The only groups of people who escaped this were those who got sick and those who exercised."

As the clouds got dark and the winds blew in the first drops of an early Spring rain, they passed the 14th street entrance again and realized that they were on the final 3/4 mile of the Peachtree road race course. They walked fast down the hill as the rain started to soak in. As Tom started to divert to his car, Sam took charge. "Hell, lets finish this thing." As this was the first time Tom and Suzi had heard Sam say such a word, they looked at one another, smiled, and followed him around the lake, breaking into a jog for 100 yds and then walking for 50-100 yds. Sam was thoroughly soaked but had a wonderful look of relaxation and accomplishment as the trio walked back to the cars.

"I'm glowing, guys, I can't beleive that we covered 3 miles!"

"Not all of us are guys," said Suzi, in a tone of voice making it clear that she was only partially joking.

"I didn't want to come out here today," said Sam, "and really had to drag myself out to meet you, uh, folks, but now I feel so good. When I walk with my wife I always feel better afterward, but when I go with you folks, I feel challenged, and energized. Thanks for getting me out here."

Suzi asked Tom about the nutrition clinic, and they shouted to Sam that it was at 9am. As the rain started to pour loudly on the top of Tom's car, Suzi yelled, "I can't wait for Breakfast at Phidippides." Tom rolled down the top of his window and Suzi confided in a lower tone of voice, "Besides, I can't wait to see one of your former flames."

* For more dietary and food information see GALLOWAY'S BOOK ON RUNNING, pp 228-246.

Saturday April 1st: 8 am
"Tom, I've discovered this great new diet! The only food I have been eating is Breyers chocolate chip mint ice cream. I want you to know that when I got on the scales this morning, I'd already lost 12 pounds in two weeks! But after eating it I have unbelievable energy and endurance— I just finished running the Peachtree course—I'm talking to you on my new car phone, purchased by frequent eater coupons on the back of the ice cream boxes. OK, I will see you at Phidippides at 11. I've already called Sam. But no bagels. I'm going to be inspired to really eat right, and that's no April Fool."

As Tom walked through the door, the speaker was sizing up the audience, asking what they wanted to get out of the session. Suzi didn't hesitate to give feedback. "I want a diet which will let me eat all the time, and still lose weight."

The speaker surprised most of the folks who were wearing a variety of running gear and jeans, as well as beautiful, coordinated running outfits. "Most of you can do both, if you change one word. Instead of focusing on losing 'weight', lets get rid of 'fat'."

Quickly glancing around the room, Tom

spotted Sam, and noticed that he wasn't nibbling on anything, so he grabbed two bagles from the refreshment table near the check-out counter. Sam declined his offer, saying he was holding out for food with more carbohy-drates—donuts. Tom decided to play a trick on him and raised his hand to ask a question. "Are donuts good sources of energy?"

The speaker looked surprised to see Tom, and obviously recognized him. Very professionally, she said "Donuts are mostly fat. Fat is a terrible source of energy, and will usually slow down digestion and make you feel lethargic for several hours. As the fat gets into the blood stream, it clogs up the system in many ways."

Somewhat unprofessionally she contin-ued "for some people this message takes years to sink in."

A few people chuckled who knew the history between Tom and the speaker, Susan.

Suzi came back to her orignival question. "What do you mean by substituting 'weight' for 'fat'? Susan explained that the scales were not a good way to gauge fat-loss because they reward you for getting dehydrated, which can lead to exhaustion, lowered resistence to disease, and lowered physical capacity. Exercise was the best way to burn off fat. She briefly explained how exercise often caused an increase in muscle size, an increase in blood plasma, and increased storage of water and non-fat energy storage for exercise. All of these things increased the body's ability to burn fat during and after exercise, but could produce a temporary increase in body weight during the first few months of exercise.

"Well how are you going to measure your fat loss then?" asked Sam.

"Through your clothes, the 'pinch' test, and your awareness of your body. If you're serious, you can have a profession monitor with regular caliper tests, but these should be done by the same person." Then Sam asked a question a "pleasantly" overweight man that he knew. "What's the best fat 'awareness' tests?" The speaker took out what she called the "high-tech" fat assessment instrument of the 17th century,"which is still the best and the most convenient, the mirror."

She explained that another expert would talk about the "burning" side of the fat equation. Her role was to explain the best foods for energy—which wouldn't let you down or bring the fat level up—and she quickly dispelled another myth, sacred to most who learn most of their nutrition information through their mother.

"Don't think that you have to eat three square meals a day. That can often lead to fat accumulation. Snacking on the right foods—even 5 to 6 times a day— can be the best way to lose fat and stay energized."

She explained how small regular meals give you the energy needed to be mentally alert and motivated, and give the body a chance to burn off what it takes in. If you get into a lifestyle of eating this way, you'll teach the body to be a better manager of what it takes in, and it'll become more efficient at burning it off. Be sure to avoid foods that have more than 20% of their calories in fat, and foods that have concentrated amounts of sugar.

"Waiting between meals is one of the best ways to store fat. The longer you wait, the more of your next meal will be stored away."

"Eating fat produces fat storage. Carbohydrates will give you the energy you need, and will only become fat if you eat too much of them. Up to 25% of your carbohydrate intake is burned up in the processing anyway—and there's a 'grace period' before fat deposition, during which the excess will be available for burnoff—in exercise."

When asked about the preferred foods, she took out her eating frequency chart which, according to Suzi, corresponded closely to Galloway's guerrilla eating guide.

"She's telling us what we were talking about the other day, that it's possible to have a continuous supply of energy throughout the day, whispered Sam, "instead of having the usual 'letdowns' in mid-morning or late afternoon. I just assumed that those were the givens of life."

After rating the priority of the topics raised in the questions at the beginning of the session, the speaker was about to start into three areas of interest: 1) An eating plan for exercise, to feel energized before and during exercise, without digestive problems or lethargy. 2) A more general eating plan which would help burn off fat, without the loss of energy, and 3) Specific foods which taste good and accomplish the goals of 1 & 2.

But she paused for questions first, to see which of these areas interested the audience. Suzi asked one that had been burning in her mind for some time.

"My body has recently betrayed me. Until I was about 25 I could eat just about anything and stay slim. Then, I started to eat more sensibly—a vegetarian diet—and that worked for a while. Suddenly, during the last 18 months I've gained a lot of fat, and my eating hasn't changed at all. What's going on?"

Susan explained how fat deposition occurs—first between the layers of muscle cells—as in the best cuts of beef. For years, Suzi was actually adding fat, but didn't know it. Only when the inside layers were filled up did the fat spill over to the surface. While Susan recommended a low fat diet which, she said, would help to keep from adding more to the body, she advised that the only way to reduce 'the fat blanket' was to exercise.

While Susan was answered a question, Suzi whispered to Tom, "at least she said that my fat was like the fat of the BEST cuts of beef. How embarassing to be compared to the ordinary cuts."

"I'm not sure I like the way this is going," said Tom. "She seems to say that we've got to take some responsibility for what we eat, what's going on here? That's no fun."

A very overweight lady started to ask a question that related to her belief that vitamins were the key ingredient for keeping people young and energetic.

"Don't put too much stock in any one type of food, and certainly not in the food supplements. There's only one thing which will tend to keep you younger than your years, and that's regular exercise. It teaches your body to use food more efficiently, and helps you stay energized. If you're looking for a 'fountain of youth' it would be related to the body's output, and not the input."

The woman who asked the question was the second most shocked person in the room. Tom chuckled "She and I argued about this for hours, and she kept telling me how limited the effects of exercise were. The chief of the nutrition police must be softening, a bit."

For at least 30 minutes after the talk, Suzi listened to Susan as individuals came up with their own questions. At one point Tom asked Suzi to meet for a walk on Saturday, and Susan interrupted her questions to say hi to him. As Tom was leaving, he heard Suzi and Susan laughting and talking, and of course supposed that they were talking about him. Sam and Tom talked by the car about the "real man's" diet of beer and polish sausages and other sins of their youth. Sam was tired and needed to go, so they decided to meet at Sandy Springs Phidippides on Saturday morning, to discuss the diet over bagels, low fat bagels.

49

Sam and Tom were standing by Tom's car when Suzi pulled up near them. Tom ushered them into the Bread Company store for some strong coffee. They watched as buses pulled up in front of the Phidippides store and unloaded passengers in running shorts and tops.

As Suzi struggled to open her PowerBar, Tom revealed that he'd entered them in a 2 mile fun-walk/run. Sam was a bit concerned about being the last person, and Tom immediately responded that this 2 miler was designed for first-time participants. The course was flat, and there was no promotion of competition.

Suzi wondered why so many people on the buses were dressed for a race. She realized that the crowd was not the typically young, thin competitors, but many were hefty and over 40. At this point, Tom had them grab their cups and board his car for the start.

This is probably the fastest 10K course in the South," said Tom. The 2 mile and the 10K are part of the **Piedmont Hospital Classic.**

When Sam asked what made a fast course "fast" Tom showed them. "The runners you saw getting out of busses parked at the finish, about 230 vertical feet lower than the start, where we had been. They drove the beautiful course which rolled along a ridgeline on Mt. Vernon Highway, and then took a wonderful downhill roll to the finish. The 2 mile was lining up as they pulled into the parking lot of the Canada Life Building. Tom was walking before he had a chance to realize he was in a "race", and therefore didn't get nervous.

As they walked out of the parking lot onto Powers Ferry Road, they passed a group of slower walkers, and Tom continued the conversation. "Tell us about your 'new' diet, Suzi."

"After talking to Susan, your ex-flame, I've decided to go on my Peachtree diet. This diet calls for avoiding a large quantity of food at one time, and lessens the time between snacks."

Sam chuckled as Suzi emphasized the "ex" part of ex-flame. "I like this racing," he said as they passed another group of walkers. When a walker ahead of them jogged for a hundred yards or so, Sam followed her lead, and Tom and Suzi, did too."

Tom continued to unlock Suzi's new

diet, which amounted to snacks of about 200-300 calories eaten every 2-3 hours or so. Yesterday, for example, she related that she ate a whole PowerBar gradually over 3 hours, and felt a steady supply of energy throughout the day. "The effect was similar to that of coffee," she said, "but I couldn't find any listing of caffeine in the ingredients."

"You can't get me to eat those things," said Sam, "they taste like sawdust."

"Yea," said Tom, "you really have to get used to them."

As they made the turn-around, Sam was really into the run/walk routine and had caught up with the woman in the lead.

Suzi and Tom continued the nutrition discussion. "It's only been a few days, but I think that I feel more 'energized', and have a steady feeling of motivation. The greatest part is that I don't have to endure long hunger spells and lapses in concentration when all I think about is food. This pattern of eating has given me the energy—and helped with the mental attitude—so that I want to burn fat. On my two walks I've eaten a PowerBar just before and felt that it boosted my blood sugar to just the right level. I must admit starvation doesn't give you the horsepower to get out there regularly.

As they rounded the final bend, Suzi and Tom noticed that Sam was still ahead of them, even though they had been taking most of the jogging breaks. They jogged the last quarter mile, with Suzi out of breath, and finished just

behind Sam who was caught up in the music, and the refreshments which were provided in the finish area. The normally low-key academician stormed right over and claimed his T-shirt.

Suzi spotted a woman she knew, and said, "Hi."

Tom noticed that the woman seemed to avoid Suzi. In an abrupt voice, she related that she had moved to Boston.

"Oh, did you know that Dylan has moved there?"

There was an awkward moment of silence, and it was clear the other woman was thinking of something else. Thankfully, for all concerned, the PA system blared the news that the 10K leaders were coming.

The rest of the morning was a joy for all, except Suzi. Just as they had settled in to their snacks, which were provided free in the finish area, it was announced that the 10K leaders were making their final approach around the Canada Life Building. Tom explained tactics to Suzi and Sam. He knew two of the competitors and guessed that the first (looking like he was a time warp from the 60's) was putting in bursts of speed before the finish, to tire out the faster one, to hopefully keep him from winning in a sprint at the end. As a third competitor moved into position to challenge the lead, Suzi nervously shouted, "Dylan, what are you doing here?"

Tom looked at Suzi, as if to say 'how do you know this guy'?

Dylan "the timewarp" gave another burst,and Tom said that it was within 300 meters of the finish, and he may be trying to steal the lead. As the competitors came in sight of the finish, the crowd roared louder when the third runner steadily moved up on Dylan, while the sprinter dropped back. Sam surprised Tom and Suzi as he cheered and ran behind the roped-off area, watching the course as it went to the finish line. Dylan looked confident with 100 meters to go, but the young runner pulled even and surprised him. Dylan strained to move ahead of him and his competitor matched his effort. The kicker took off at this point and was closing the gap quickly. Dylan was really straining now, pulling ahead and then being caught. All three demonstrated three different styles of running, each at the top of their form. Even while straining, Dylan was smooth and strong. But the kicker was stronger and everyone knew that he would have no trouble passing the others as he came up on them with 30 meters to go. As they approached the narrowing entrance to the finish chute, Dylan sensed the power of his competitor from behind and forced him over to the edge. At the very last moment, the kicker cut his stride to avoid a corner of the finish chute, because Dylan had forced him off the course. The older competitor leaned at the tape and won by an inch or less.

Sam was stunned by the sudden outcome of the race, and the tricks pulled at the end. Tom sensed this and said, "It was a dirty victory, but still a victory." Suzi didn't say a word, but watched as Dylan walked out of the chute, raised his hands up towards the sky, and looked around. Tom noticed that Suzi's face changed color and appearance instantly as a woman came up and hugged him. On second glance, Tom realized that she was the same woman with whom Suzi had spoken earlier. When Tom asked her what happened, Suzi didn't say a word, but seemed to be in shock.

Sam watched as wave after wave of runners came in, exhilarated by their fast times. Almost 90 per cent of the field qualified for up-front seeding at the Peachtree Road Race. He was particularly impressed with the expressions on their faces. Whereas many had a look of concentration, almost everyone was pleasant, with an interesting focus which varied from person to person. "Each face tells its own story" he said to Tom, who barely heard as he wandered off to find Suzi.

Tom was still looking as he passed by the awards stage, where Dylan was explaining his race to a small group of younger runners. He caught Tom's eye and said:

"Well, Burke, It's been so long since I beat you in a race that I figured you had gotten fat and smart, It's tough getting beaten all the time, isn't it?"

Anger and irritation caused Tom's mind to unleash a complex stream of messages, emotions, and memories. There were only 3 people he had met in his 20 years of running who had made Tom feel this way, and one was standing in front of him. Even Dylan could sense this.

"You know I'm kidding, Burke—just the exuberance of victory—that sort of thing."

Tom managed to settle into his business mode, which he used when dealing with the big egos of difficult clients.

"I've just started back to help a friend prepare for Peachtree."

Dylan tried, in his next statement, to be supportive. "You know, I'm looking forward to the time when I can drop out of this competitive stuff also, but turning forty offers a new wave of trophies and sometimes, prize money."

Tom spotted Suzi heading for her car in the next parking lot, and ran to talk to her. She didn't say anything as Tom thanked her for the suggestion about coming to the race. Sam joined them still turned on by the event.

He related how the woman he ran with was part of a marathon training group (like the one Suzi had mentioned). She ran with them each weekend at their easy and comfortable pace. The group leader made everyone take the one minute walking breaks, even though they didn't want to in the beginning. This woman had never run a step before starting the program, and had just finished the Charlotte Observer Marathon. While she had lost 13 pounds, she had gained a sense of confidence which she'd never experienced in her life. Sam said that his feeling at the end of the 2 mile gave him a brief glimpse into this world, and he liked it. "I thought these 5K's and 10K's were just for the skinny, super fit athletes—but most of the folks looked like me. You know, over the hill. I really didn't know how alive I could feel."

Suzi was seated in her car, looking depressed and not talking. Tom took action, pulled her from the car and told her that she was going to join Sam and him on a "warm-down."

Tom took the conversational lead, again, explaining how important the warm-down was after any hard effort. Then he told about seeing his former competitor, Dylan. Sensing something, he asked Suzi how she knew him. Suzi changed the subject at the first opportunity, when the first woman finished the race.

Not far behind the first woman who finished came Timmy Jacobs, a little kid who passed 3 adults in the final 100 meters. Twenty meters before the finish, Timmy passed the tallest runner in the race, 6'5" Jack Tornwell and the scene was memorable. Nine-year-old Timmy was probably one third the height of Jack, who had been a good high school track athlete a decade ago. For the next mile they discussed whether running was beneficial for kids.

The exercise seemed to loosen Suzi up. She first congratulated Sam on "getting the bug." Then she opened up about the winner of today's Piedmont Hospital Classic.

"Dylan is the guy I visited in Boston, when I met you guys on the plane. He's been giving me all these stories about 'needing to start a new dating life in Boston,' that we needed a 'break from one another.' The woman with him today was my roommate last year. We double dated a lot. Judging from what I saw, they are definitely starting a new life, together. It wouldn't be so bad if either of them had just been honest about it."

Tom related how Dylan treated him as a has-been, in a condescending way. "He's right, I've gained weight, let my conditioning go, and I feel bad about that. But the way he talked to me. I want to get back into shape and put him in his place. I'm probably mad mostly because he is doing what I want to do—down deep—getting back to competition."

Sam's aristocratic southern drawl led them to believe that a philosophical statement was about to come, but he surprised them. "It appears that it might be time to invoke an ancient, time-tested Southern tradition, "Get back into training, Tom, and whip his ass."

54

The ride back to Sandy Springs Phidippides was so lively the trio had to finish the conversation in the Bread Company, over tea and a muffin or two. An argument erupted when Suzi assumed that the muffins were low in fat, and Sam didn't think so. It was good that Suzi ate her muffin early, because when she went to get a tea refill, and to ask about the ingredients, she noticed Susan, the nutritionist, walk in. The expert, with some reluctance, agreed to intercede.

"Most muffins have a good bit of fat in them, some have over 50% of their calories in fat."

Sam, feeling good at being 'right,' followed up with a question that had been bothering him.

"How does the fat you eat get deposited around the arteries?"

Susan qualified her answer by saying that she'd only done a little work in the bio-chemistry area on fat, but was pleased to tell what she knew. She went on to issue the standard academician's disclaimer. "This is a very complicated process which I don't like to even try to simplify."

She explained that when the body stores of fat are at least 20% higher than 'normal' the fat stays longer in the bloodstream. Tom broke in accusing the offending fat of " loitering and causing trouble."

"Yes," said Susan, "because a diet which is high in fat will allow for this 'sludge' to be 'loitering' around the arteries, attaching itself to the walls, and to other fat which has already been stuck there. After years of this build-up, the blockages occur."

"Does exercise help, even for an obese person with a fatty diet? Does exercise help?" asked Tom.

"Oh, yes. There are two types of lipo-proteins in the blood stream, high density and low density. Regular, endur-ance exercisers have more of the high density types, which tend to bounce off the walls. The low density lipo-proteins are the offenders which stick to the sides of the arteries and can eventually cause death."

"I heard what you said at Phidippides, about vitamins," said Sam, "but aren't there any vitamins which might improve health or reduce disease?"

"My reaction was based upon a continu-ing notion in the 'fad food press' that you can take a pill which will take care of any problem," responded the nutritionist. "The more I'm in this field, the more I realize that exercise does much more for long-term health than diet. But a terrible diet can lead to heart disease and other problems, even in extremely fit people."

"Do you take vitamins?" asked Suzi.

Susan's Anti-Oxidant Supplement Program

400 IU of Vitamin E
500 mg of Vitamin C
25,000 IU of Beta Carotene (Vitamin A)

"I take an antioxidant supplement," said Susan. "Dr.Kenneth Cooper of the Aerobics Institute believes that those who are engaged in heavy exercise, especially anaerobic work, should probably double the amount which I take."

"Can you eat too little fat?" asked Suzi.

"It's hard to tell at this time. Moderation is always the key to dietary change. Never change dramatically. Through gradually cutting down on harmful substances, you can develop a healthy and energetic lifestyle eating plan. It's always better to avoid animal fat. But if you've reduced your dietary fat to less than 20% of total calories, you can occasionally enjoy a bowl of ice cream, or a muffin, Suzi."

Galloway's Guerrilla Guide to Foods that keep you FILLED...but keep off the FAT

Non-fat (or very low fat) bulk foods can give you the complex carbohydrates your body needs—with enough fiber to keep you from getting hungry for a while. By preparing them in advance, and having sauces or flavorings readily available, you can prepare healthy "fast" food—when you want it. By filling up on these healthy fiber foods before you get hungry, you'll have a steady supply of energy and blood sugar throughout the day—and won't tend to over-eat. Keep experimenting with seasonings to give maximum variety.

The Staples...which fill you up
*Pasta * Potatoes * Brown Rice

During a period when you have the time available (most do this on weekends), cook up enough of each to last about a week. Keep the supply in your refrigerator. It only takes a few minutes before mealtime to heat up the staples, add seasonings, and eat.

The "Fill-Ins"...which add nutrition, substance, and variety
* Frozen Vegetables   * Lean Protein (chicken, turkey, fish) * Fresh Vegetables/ Beans

It helps to cook the protein in advance also. By putting the protein and vegetables in the sauce for several hours before your meal, the flavor is enhanced.

Seasonings..which make it taste good
* Low-fat pasta sauce   * Low-fat soup mixes
* Non-fat salad dressings * Your own

Breads & Croutons...for "crunch"

* Whole-grain breads   * Toasted slices of breads, rolls   * Very low-fat chips

Snacks..keep eating to maintain energy and avoid over-eating at the next meal

* PowerBars * Fat-Free Saltines *Fat-Free or Lo- Fat Pretzels   * Bagels

Drink water all day long. Remember that drinks with sugar (including fruit juices) will often add fat or maintain it—because of the concentrated sugar.

After laughing a good bit, throwing out thoughts about Suzi and   Dylan, and then the proposed rivalry between Tom and Dylan, the conversation shifted to the subject of children's running.

Sam was impressed with the very fast performance of the 9-year-old who ran the Piedmont Hospital 10K course in 41:10.

During the time that the three had observed him, Timmy was well mannered, related well to adults, and seemed to genuinely enjoy running and competition. "Looks like we have a future Olympian here," said Sam.

"That is, IF he's still running by the time he reaches Olympic age," said Suzi. "Before the age of 18 most kids have problems dealing with the complex human emotions associated with success—Is it trophies, praise from adults, rewards from the parents?"

Tom agreed, relating how he wanted so much for his son Chris to follow in his footsteps. From age 6-10 he was in a kids' running program, with a teddy bear-type coach. While the coaches didn't seem to put pressure on the kids, Tom now realized that the kids did it to themselves.

"I remember another father who also wanted his kid, Tim, to run, but held him back, allowing him to run only in a few races, and only when he really wanted to do so. Tim played soccer and got in great shape through that sport.

"Two races stand out in my mind when Tim and Chris met. At age 7, in a 100-meter all comers race, the starter told each child to stay in his lane all the way. But when the gun fired, two kids sprinted in front of Tim and Chris. The track coaches had taught Chris to stay in his lane, so he waited until he had an opening in his lane and then passed the other runner. Tim instinctively moved to another lane and won the race.

"Chris had trouble dealing with that loss. Even at age 7, Chris had learned by reading between the lines—and from other kids—that he was on a track team and he was expected to WIN the race, or exhaust himself trying. Tim just seemed to get out there and *run*.

"Then, when both Tim and Chris were 10, they entered the Miracle Mile. There were prizes for age groups, which was promoted heavily during Chris's track practice. Tim had been playing a lot of soccer with only a little running in his PE classes. Chris had been working out hard, probably as an escape and a refuge from the marital problems which his mother and I were going through. Tim went out at a reasonable pace, just behind the leaders. My son went fast—as he was told by team coaches—to get a good position. Half-way through the race, Tim caught up with Chris, and Chris sensed this so he accelerated. As they approached the finish, Tim slowly accelerated until the two were side by side. I could see that Chris was straining, and that Tim was enjoying being in the hunt. They ran stride for stride to the finish, each giving it everything he could, and Chris out-leaned Tim.

"Chris never seemed to have an attraction for running after that—even though he won the race. I will never forget that after the race, Tim had this look on his face—as if a whole new world had opened up. Tim was the one who finished second in that Piedmont Hospital race today."

"Running is such an introspective activity," said Suzi, "and that's why it is so great for adults as a stress reliever, to get right-brain relief from left brain activity. But kids can overload their circuits too easily and get mentally burned out."

"You see," continued Suzi, "kids can get swept along into the inner spaces, and push beyond their limits. Not only does this produce mental fatigue, it brings with it mental projections and expectations which are unrealistic. Later, when they don't live up to these artificial 'promises,' children lose confidence in themselves, without the capacity to understand what's going on."

"The physical scars are bad enough," noted Tom, "but mental scars take a lot longer to heal."

"The spirit of a child is very delicate," said Sam. "Too much of a good activity, too soon, can lead to burnout, even when the child seems to be involved. But when a young and vibrant spirit is gently molded into positive areas, it responds, by enhancing the growth of the whole person."

Tom shook himself awake as the plane landed, gathered his stuff from the overhead rack, and made his way to the baggage claim area. He looked at his watch as he was leaving the cashier at the long-term parking, 7:02 am. He first considered a wide range of excuses to get out of his "team walk" with Sam and Suzi at 9 am. But as he drove along the relatively quiet, Saturday morning freeway, he realized that it was possible to go home, check the mail over coffee, and meet Sam and Suzi for their scheduled rendezvous at Phidippides-Ansley. As he paused after putting water on the stove and dropping his bag off in the bedroom, the bed seemed to be pulling him in that direction like a giant electromagnet pulls a huge hunk of iron. He mistakenly told himself that he would "rest his eyes" for only a few minutes, and instantly he became one with the bed, in the oblivion called fatigue.

The phone jolted Tom into reality. It was Suzi, checking up on him before leaving for Phidippides. Tom begged for a holiday—but she wouldn't budge. With that established, Tom negotiated for one of her "quick-fix" motivation visualizations. While not wild about doing this over the phone, Suzi reluctantly agreed.

"Imagine that you are a steam engine. The boiler right now is just starting to put out steam, but the pressure is building, now it is pushing strongly against the pistons that drive your legs. You're standing up, and the pressure is starting to flow through your body, you're moving easier and easier as the system gets up to speed."

At the mention of "steam," Tom felt a twinge of anxiety, which grew, as the visualization continued, into a deep, sinking feeling.

He quickly told Suzi he'd be there, hung up and bolted into the kitchen, where a strong burning smell led him to the tea kettle, which had boiled dry and then melted on the stove. This jolted him awake as he cleaned up the mess, grabbed his mail, and headed for the nearest Starbucks for the strongest coffee they could brew. While waiting for a dose of espresso to be mixed into the coffee of the day, Tom picked out a letter from Pensacola from the pile of mostly junk mail which had gathered during his trip. The adrenaline gave him the "jump start" he needed. He tore open the envelope.

Dear Tom,

I know it's unusual for me to write, beyond my obligatory Christmas card each year, but here goes. As is my style, I'll get immediately to the point. Chris is moving to Atlanta. I don't expect you to be overjoyed—or even to come and see him often— I just wanted you to know. But I did want to ask a big favor.

First, a little background. After managing lawyers' offices for 13 years, I shifted into doctors' office management. It was a great career opportunity, and the pay increase was also significant. At first, I worked handling the billing and clerical work for a group of cardiologists. When two of them spun off to set up a rehab and preventive clinic I went with them and managed their operation with a fitness center. Imagine me, the anti-exercise princess, around the gym, full-time.

During the past 3 years, your son Chris has been doing some cross country running. It started when a couple of his friends joined the team, and after a few meets, everyone found out that Chris was good (no surprise to me, considering his father). He did well, winning some smaller races, but never doing well in the big meets. (No surprise to me, considering his father). Sorry to say so, but we know it's true. Last year was Chris's senior year and a bad one for him. He decided not to go to college, and this has been a year "in limbo." His running has kept him on track, more or less, as he has taken a variety of part-time jobs.

Tom, I know that I hurt you when I told you that I needed to raise Chris in my own environment, and I still believe that I was right in that decision. But I made some big mistakes in not letting Chris be more a part of your life. You have been great through these years now, and I'd like for Chris to see the positive attributes of his father. It is becoming apparent to me now that the forced separation which I imposed may have increased his desire to get to know you. The truth is, he puts you way up there on a pedestal.

A person from my office just relocated to Atlanta, and will be working at Peachtree Hospital. He found an entry level technical job for Chris—the same job Chris has been doing here, part-time. Chris will be staying with this friend Bill Collins and his wife in the Morningside area.

Now for the favor. I don't even know whether you are still running, but I think I know the answer to that. I would love for you to spend a little time with Chris, take him for a run, go to a running store (is Phidippides still in Ansley Mall?) or something. He's a bit on the shy side, but he has a quiet strength which I know you'll like. I'll call to follow up.

Gloria

Tom looked for something to divert attention away from his tardiness as he walked into the Phidippides store, and noticed that Sam was wearing a pair of ancient and ragged hiking shorts, and a 30+ year old Wyndham University sweatshirt. But at least he did have on his new running shoes.

"Hey Sam, I see you found the vintage Wyndham University running wear section of the store." And then he suggested looking around for something lighter and more comfortable. Sam replied that at his level of 'maturity' and body shape, and the skimpiness of the latest exercise fashions, he felt much more comfortable in the clothes he had on.

Suzi noted that if Tom had arrived when he'd promised, the temperature would have been 15 degrees cooler, and then added, "No guilt intended."

As they moved toward the door of the store, Sam asked Tom about his trip to the West Coast.

Tom explained that his business discussions had gone well with several insurance companies, that he had to take the "red-eye" and that his cup of Starbucks' strongest was just beginning to take effect. He also noted that a strong reality check had arrived in the mail while he was gone.

As the guys were trying to leave the store, Suzi looked over the flyer rack with its smorgasbord of information on fun runs, races, camps and other fitness opportunities. She told Tom that she would pry herself away from the flyers, if he would

Galloway's Guerrilla Guide:
Motivation: Framing Your Experience

By giving a simple, meaningful purpose to several experiences a year, you offer challenges which can be interesting and non-intimidating. If the goal is not achieved, it doesn't take anything away from the fitness experience, the fun, or any other benefits of the program. Most runners use races to frame their challenges.

Challenge Another Person
It helps to challenge people who can help bring out the motivation, in a friendly way. I have enjoyed staying in touch with several friends with whom I ran 25+ years ago, particularly Frank Shorter and Bill Rodgers. I may not beat them, but if one of them is scheduled to attend an event where I will be, the challenge is on.

Challenge A Younger You
A few years ago, I celebrated the 30th anniversary of my first marathon—with a goal of running faster than I had in my first one. While I had not run that time in several years (2:56), I felt that it was possible. More important, I knew that I could do it without the aches and pains I had experienced as an 18-year-old. In spite of an ankle problem, I ran even pace toward the goal for the first half—and then took 6 minutes off my 18-year-old time during the second half. Indeed, I felt great during the afternoon and evening—with almost no aches and pains.

Endurance Frames
One of the great satisfactions of fitness is feeling the specific accomplishment of increasing your long run—every two weeks or so. The walking breaks can be increased in frequency and duration so that you can "frame" for yourself a half-marathon, or even a marathon, within the next 12 months—with low risk of aches and injury.

Avoid "Personal Best" Frames
While top performance goals can be structured in a different way, the "framing" process is designed to set yourself up for success and fun. A difficult time goal leaves most of the fun out of the frame—and is not recommended.

tell her what he meant about the "reality check" he had received in his mail. Tom replied that he needed another cup of coffee, recommending that they adjourn to the Ansley Mall coffee shop. Suzi grabbed three copies of the free Phidippides/Galloway training program for Peachtree, purchased a 6 pack of PowerBars, and headed for the Java house.

As they sat with cups in hand, Tom seemed to absorb inspiration from the contents in his cup. He told Sam and Suzi about the letter, and that he was uneasy about his son Chris coming to Atlanta, and questioned whether he could really relate to Chris, but that he was also looking forward to getting to know him. Suzi passed around the PowerBars.

"This one energy tip, which your ex-friend Susan expounded upon, has been the best food for maintaining energy throughout the day. Tom, it really works for me. I'm still not sure that I like the taste—except for, maybe, the new mocha or the banana flavor."

When Tom started to unleash a series of skeptical comments, Suzi assured him that he shouldn't taint the product just because Susan recommended it. Tom laughed. "At this point, I will take anything that works, to open the eyes and build my motivation just to get out there."

"Even when I eat it with water, the effect of the PowerBar is similar to that of caffeine," said Suzi. "I've started using them on my busy days. Between clients I can take a few bites and be energized for another hour, without getting the 'blood sugar blues'."

Sam mumbled the ingredients list, "Brown rice, oat bran, fructose. This is the diet of *my* client, ancient man."

"It reminds me of several articles from SCHOOL WEEKLY about 6th or 7th grade—telling what the astronauts were going to eat—ground-up food in convenient forms," added Tom.

"This has got to be 'good for you'," said Sam, after biting into the chewy product, and using a strong cup of coffee to wash it down.

As they played with their food, the Peachtree training program became the main topic of conversation. Sam confided that while he was still exhilarated after the Piedmont Hospital Classic the previous weekend, he felt overwhelmed. The training program was just what he needed to see what he was doing. It gives my left brain, the logical side, a massage.

"Most comforting for me is the ability to do the work noted on that day, cross it off, and stay on track. It seems very realistic. Even a total 'couch potato' like myself can feel comfortable walking 30 minutes, every other day. The only increase occurs on the weekend long runs. After doing those walking breaks this weekend, I know that I can get to that Peachtree finish line."

* For extensive 10K schedules see GALLOWAY'S BOOK ON RUNNING

The confidence seemed to build from

within as they each pulled energy from one other. Tom confessed that when he had arrived at the coffee shop, he was beginning to feel that his goal of giving Dylan a scare at Peachtree was not very realistic. But now that the PowerBar was kicking in—he was ready to get out there.

"You're 'framing your goal'," explained Suzi. "When I work with clients who are trying to get back on track after time away from career, studies, etc., I have to keep them from comparing themselves with what they were doing at another place, another time. By putting the goal in the proper 'frame,' you can have both a meaningful challenge, and a great chance at success."

Tom admitted that she had just articulated one of his major motivational problems. Every time he tried to get back into running, he couldn't "frame it" as fitness or fun, or as Galloway put it, "Transcendental." The challenge with Dylan was real to him, and meaningful. With this experience "framed," it no longer mattered how fast he ran, or that his current times were not as fast as he had run at his best.

"I should take a frame with me on every workout, frame each step,"said Suzi, "and then go home to work on the next frame on this schedule tomorrow."

As the pieces of PowerBar and the coffee disappeared, the trio headed out the door. Since she resided in the Midtown area, Suzi had picked a beautiful course which led through Piedmont Park. She was also the drill instructor in reverse, enforcing a 2-3 minute walking break

after every 1-2 minutes of running.

As they left the Ansley Mall parking lot, Sam asked Tom to tell more about his work. After giving a "boiler plate" job description, Tom editorialized for his companions.

"The owner of the company started an insurance company with some of his church friends 15 years ago. It was their theory to draw only from religious people, speculating that this would reduce the risk. It didn't work out, but he discovered pockets of business; many companies didn't want to spend time producing company picnics and other special events, for example. He built a great corporate events business just from friends he had met in the insurance business.

"I was hired 9 years ago, when a few of the larger, self-insured companies started asking for programs which might help their employees reduce cardiovascular disease by improving fitness and eating habits. Out of several options, they chose a team-building format. As an exercise specialist, I wanted to produce scientifically-designed programs which could target those at risk, and track progress of anyone in the program. I was much too idealistic. Most of the companies only wanted a fitness club "perk" for top execs, or "fun and games" for employees. I've tried to get the boss up to speed on this, but it is happening very slowly."

"You may get some help from the insurance industry," said Suzi. "When I renegotiated insurance policies last month for my company, several agents told me that there were some major incentive programs being designed—to encourage prevention—both among employees and companies, because everyone wins when people are fit and healthy."

"That's what I discussed with the guys on the West Coast this past week. After 10 years of seeing similar data, they are finally ready to admit that even low levels of regular exercises—walking for example—lowers the chance of long-term, expensive health problems. It also increases productivity, and improves attitude. Keeping your employees healthy is about the only way that companies are going to restrain the increase in health and life insurance costs, as the population ages. And there are so many other benefits on top of all this. Of course, it has to be organized and targeted to be most effective."

Tom went on the describe how the current climate for HMO's is to cut costs, in order to gain market share. All of the HMO's and insurance companies he met with were interested in his products, but felt that they were about three (cost-cutting) years away from real prevention programs.

"All of these companies are merging or thinking about it. Nobody knows who they will be reporting to a year from now—or whether they will be at the same company. It's hard to plan for the long term under those conditions. But the company who does this will be ahead of the pack."

Sam started too fast, and was huffing and puffing after the first few "jogs."

When his heart monitor started to buzz, Suzi slowed the pace down. After about half a mile at the slower pace, Suzi could sense that Tom was getting impatient. When she told him to go ahead and pick up the pace, he declined at first. After a while, however, Tom was getting fired up about his Dylan Challenge, and accepted, striking out on his own during the last lap. Even with their untrained eyes, Suzi and Sam could tell that Tom looked strong and efficient as he took off and glided into the distance.

"Doesn't it detract from the workout when you slow down and lower the heart rate during a series of walking breaks, as in this workout?" asked Suzi.

"At Junaluska, I asked about this several times," answered Suzi. "I even looked into some of the fitness research. If you are moving forward continuously by walking or running, as opposed to stopping at regular intervals, you are using massive groups of muscles, which burns 50-100 calories per mile and gives a great workout. The target heart rate is not an issue for those who just want to finish the Peachtree. Even those who are time-goal oriented could benefit from walking breaks on long runs. Some recent research showed that low levels of activity, such as light housework, provided some conditioning and a protective effect from heart disease. As I understand it, Sam, you and I can use total mileage as our measurement device. The further we go, the more benefit we receive. That's another reason why it's better to go slow early in the workout."

"I was amazed to find that about 20% of

those in the Galloway Marathon training groups—hundreds of folks each year— had never run a step in their lives, before starting the program," continued Suzi. "Six months later they are marathoners. Only by taking walking breaks could these people accomplish this."

Sam and Suzi slowed down, running one minute and walking 2-3 minutes— which allowed Sam to get back to Ansley Mall without the huffing and puffing he had experienced early in the run.

All three were feeling great at the end of the run. Suzi noticed that Tom seemed to be glowing as he finished up in front of the store.

"Once I started running continuously, it felt like I was taking off—liberated from the petty things, such as my burnt kettle—to more major things, like dealing with my long lost son's arrival in town.

"The feeling I had during the run made me feel timeless. I brought back feelings that I had, running as a teenager, coping with the hormonal imbalances, always finishing the run feeling good about myself, ready to go on. As a young adult, confronting the insecurity of marriage mistakes and divorce, I would sort out the issues on the run and the problems and come back feeling stable and strong. There's something chemical about this. The problems are still there, I just know that they are solvable, that I am equal to them."

Sam confessed that he was surprised at the way he felt. "The apprehensions were beginning to really set in this morning, I actually got nervous and started to make an excuse to leave Phidippides before you came, Tom. I didn't feel equal to the task, but now a wave of confidence and composure has me rolling toward the welcome shore that is Peachtree. I'm not there yet, but suddenly have this confidence that I used to have as a young man. I cannot deny the fact that I feel better than I have felt in years, alive, successful, mentally alert, and definitely tired, but good tired!"

"I'm still not sure about these PowerBars, though."

IS THE HEART RATE MONITOR REALLY A LEFT BRAIN ALARM?

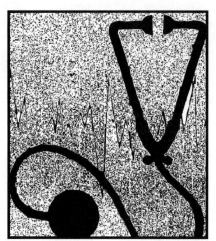

Over a bottle of Gatorade, Tom asked Sam about his heart rate monitor. As Sam went through all of the functions which he had learned, Tom confessed that he enjoyed playing with equipment like this, that he was a "closet gadget junkie." Sam's monitor was a high-tech device with a transmitter which recorded his heart rate at a central location and sent immediate notices of irregularities to Dr. Life's office.

Tom and Sam went inside to compare Sam's medical version with the over-the-counter models in Phidippides. Except for the high-tech transmitter, most of the functions were the same. Tom was surprised to find that the Phidippides staff person was almost trying not to sell the devices.

"For most runners and walkers, the heart monitor is too much. It really doesn't give enough meaningful feedback to justify the cost."

When Tom and Sam asked who could benefit from them, she went on.

"■ If you use a heart rate monitor, you must have a maximum heart rate test done, under supervision of a competent organization or institution. Whenever you push your heart to maximum capacity, there is some risk, and this should be monitored.

■ The maximum heart rate tables shouldn't be used if you have a heart rate monitor. They are averages, and the error factor can lead to significant overtraining.

■ Most runs should be done at 70% of your max heart rate, or less. The monitor will help you to stay below that figure, and keep you from overtraining, especially on easy days.

■ Turn off the monitor during the first two-thirds of your long runs (whatever is longer than you've been running during the last 2-3 weeks). The 'two minute rule' applies here. Run two minutes per mile slower than you could run that distance on that day. But turn the monitor on during the last part of the run, to keep from going over 70% as your legs get tired.

The major benefit received from the heart monitor, for most folks, is the ability to tell when you're working too hard on easy days. Most feel great when they start, and exercise too hard. This leads to dramatic slowdown and discouragement later."

"It also cuts back on the fat burning," noted Tom. "If you have to cut back on your workout, you're reducing the fat burning which could be done that session. If you are exercising within yourself, your prime time for fat-burning is at the end of the workout."

"It's a left-brain alarm," interjected Suzi, who had pretended to be looking at the new colors of women's tops and jogbras, but was soaking in every word.

When "the boys" asked her what she meant, Suzi went into the war that goes on between left and right brain when humans are under stress.

"There is a wall between the two sides, and they don't connect directly. The left side is the center of logical thought, mathematics, business, etc. But it is also the lazy brain with a million logical excuses as to why you can't do something. This excuse mechanism is probably designed to protect you from over exerting, but it overdoes its job. 'It's too hot. It's too cold, too early, too late. Why are you doing this. You could be relaxing' (eating, drinking, etc.)."

"Physical stress will activate the left brain, but so will stress from work, family, and other areas of life. So when you're tired and stressed at the end of work, it's natural to have the left brain try to keep you from doing the thing which would relieve that stress."

"Enough of that negative left brain. What about the right brain?" asked Sam.

Suzi explained that she had experienced some major breakthroughs when her clients were successful in shifting into the right brain. "It is the source of a million creative solutions to any problem."

She went on to say that the right side is quiet and doesn't try to counterattack the strong aggressive messages of the left side. But when you are able to shift under its control, it relaxes and restores, opening up creative solutions when the logical ones just didn't work. The best ways to shift into this side are through participation in activities which naturally use the right brain. One of the best is running, but cruising and walking are also productive; the right brain is activated by steady, repetitive activities which are continued for at least 15 minutes. Suzi's experience showed that the maximum effect of right brain activity seemed to start really 'clicking in' after 45 minutes.

For more information on left brain and right brain, see the Mind Power chapter in this book.

"OK, I see what you mean about the 'left brain alarm,'" said Tom. "Treadmill tests on athletes showed that they intuitively recognized the increase in stress as their heart rate rose—it was directly related. I guess this means that if we correct early when the rate goes above 70% of max, we stand a chance of keeping the stress lower throughout, and staying in the right brain, and also in the fat burning zone."

The woman who was helping them with the heart monitor had to work with a shoe customer. Tom said that he had lost interest in doing hard workouts during the past few years, because he went from feeling normal to feeling terrible, in just a few strides. Not only did the left brain go wild, the muscles rebelled. Another Phidippides staff person overheard and said that he was probably not warmed up enough for hard running in the workout and that he pushed himself too hard, too soon.

Suzi said that she had worked with clients who tried to push themselves too soon in other life projects and developed similar symptoms. She recommended lowering the intensity of the workout by running slower, taking more rest between the fast segments, shortening the fast segments, etc.

Sam said he hated to keep Suzi in a "Doctor is In" role, but he could use a motivational boost. Sam described how he consistently returned home from work feeling bad physically and mentally. When Suzi asked him to note the major problems, he listed job uncertainty, negative personality interaction at work, and his concern with what the future held for him and his family. He knew that exercise would help him feel better, but thinking about the negative list often paralyzed him from getting out there.

Suzi talked him through the relaxation session, saying that its most powerful role was to clean the mental slate so that he could start over by doing something for himself.

"How can I do something for myself, when I am preoccupied with anxiety related to what I will be doing next year?"

"Sam, do you remember the session we had about constructing a belief environment? You have to keep working on a series of beliefs about your exercise lifestyle:

- that it is good for you

- that you are designed to do it

- that it is part of you

- that if you come back from your walk or run with a good attitude, you and your family will be better off today, and that's what's important *today*."

Tom explained that he often got so involved in a project at work that he continued to work on it until it was dark, and he had no motivation left to exercise.

"Even when I break away from work by 6 pm, I can't turn my mind off. Some projects are so compelling to me that I don't want to focus on anything else. I just keep going over and over the possibilities and outcomes."

Suzi explained that our emotional responses to various situations can get very complex. The best strategy is to focus on a simple procedure in which each step leads to the next, and each helps the body and mind strip away another left brain activity level.

Sam was pretty mellowed out by the time Suzi finished with her recommendations. Tom was beginning to understand that he was not exercising because he was not choosing to take command

Steps reducing Left Brain Activity

1. Relaxation exercise.
2. Clear all thoughts—at least the negative or preoccupational ones.
3. Rehearse the positive experience of exercise—and specific good feelings from specific workouts
4. Eliminate the "pressure". Lower any expectations from exercise—erase the anticipated discomfort.
5. Start moving, slowly.

were any other major benefits from working with the device.

The Phidippidean looked at the event calendar on the wall and said that they were in luck. There was a form clinic set up for the following Wednesday—which would include some innovative form improvement techniques. The heart monitor was probably the best device for helping one to find more efficient ways of running faster with less stress.

Suzi, having forgotten her bag of PowerBars, slipped back into the store and overheard the mention of running faster. She looked at the Phidippides advisor and said, pointing to Tom, "He'll be there. He's looking for every way to beat his rival at Peachtree!"

Tom did not argue.

over his environment after work. Suzi gave him some ideas how he could do this.

As they walked out, Tom found the heart rate monitor expert who had helped him earlier and asked if there

With coffee cup in hand, Tom arrived at Phidippides just before opening. Suzi was sitting in her car listening to some new wave music, and soon joined him outside the store, offering part of her PowerBar to dunk in the coffee. Tom confessed that he only came to this session to learn the connection between heart monitor and better form. As for the other ways of improving form, he didn't believe that there was anything that he could learn, having used about every technique you could imagine in his 25 years of running. "I'm an old dog," Tom admitted.

As they waited for the speaker to hook up the video unit, Sam arrived and asked Tom to tell him whether he had been able to construct any programs for the insurance companies based upon his meetings of a week ago.

"We just started putting together some proposals for their clients which involve a network of team leaders who track and reward employee fitness. One of the companies had started this a few years ago—with team-building as the goal. One of the assigned 'team' functions was data collection. Fortunately, we set up the data systems so that they were simple to collect and sort—but this was only an afterthought and not ever expected to be used by itself. Then a new healthcare director came in 6 months ago, and was excited to find they had data on how costs related to fitness and preventive activities. When he analyzed it he found a significant reduction of costs and health problems among those who exercised regularly. He wants to look at options for expanding this. They are starting to offer 'health dividend' discounts which has started a mini boom of health promotion efforts. The insurance company sold more insurance, the companies reduced their costs, and some even gave the savings back to their healthy employees as a reward. Now the other companies are trying to catch up."

When Sam pinned him down about the insurance issues, Tom explained that one of the new insurance products is a Medical Savings Account. Employees are rewarded for staying healthy by either a cash payment at the end of the year, or special prizes such as travel or merchandise. The rewards are based not only on the reduction of medical claims, but on reporting for preventive check-ups, including treadmill and cholesterol tests. The greatest reduction in costs has been experienced by being able to target those at high risk, and to monitor and activate them to reduce the risk.

"It's my job to find a way for everyone to win. Over the next 5-10 years the insurance companies will be looking to sponsor corporate events which emphasize health promotion and prevention, like the Office Depot Event Series, which targets corporations.

"So, did you get the business, Tom?" asked Suzi.

"That's what my boss keeps asking. No. We are moving toward some discussions of the fee structure, so I know that it will happen. My boss is getting anxiety attacks about this. He doesn't understand it, and feels that he will lose control or something. He's trying to pressure me to get it done or abandon it. I know that this is the way of the future, but he has no patience for it."

With the video unit in place, the presenter began, noting that he was using Jeff Galloway's method of video form analysis. Each member of the clinic was taped, from the side, as he or she ran alongside the camera. He looked for three aspects of form which indicated the relative efficiency and use of strength resources of each runner. As he showed the playback, the clinician slowed down to a frame-by-frame look at posture, bounce and overstride.

Suzi had the best posture, with both Tom and Sam displaying a slight forward lean. Tom tended to lean only at push-off, whereas Sam leaned most of the time he was running. Sam was pleased to find out that by straightening up, he could probably reduce the tiredness in his back and neck, a natural byproduct of forward lean.

Galloway's Guerrilla Guide
POSTURE, BOUNCE, & OVERSTRIDE

POSTURE: Relaxed and Upright

Don't try to be a Marine, at attention. The best posture for running, walking or cruising is just good posture, with all elements relaxed and balanced as the foot comes underneath. A forward lean forces you to shorten your stride, and creates extra tension on the lower back and neck. A backward lean is unusual, but will also produce a shorter stride, loss of power from the running stride, and possible tension in the lower back.

Some will argue that a forward lean will help you run faster, but I've found this to help only for a hundred yards or so. It forces you to work harder, and therefore spends resources which are not available later in the run—causing you to lose more time than you gained during the short burst. The only exception I've found to this rule is when running on a gradual, downhill grade. A slight forward lean can help you run faster, and the boost from downhill gravity will offset the decrease in stride length. By having this slight monitor on downhill stride length one can help counter the negative effect of overstriding—a temptation when running downhill.

CORRECTING FORWARD LEAN—by becoming a puppet on a string

Create a mental image, during the form drill, you are suspended, from the very top of your head, by a giant string, (as if you were a puppet). The effect is to lift you upright—head in line with shoulders, with hips and everything lined up with cach foot as it assumes the body's weight. A "good puppet" also helps you to stay light on your feet.

The first effect of being a "good puppet" is to have your body line up without any tension—you're in balance. Walk around with the image of the puppet on the string, until you feel relaxed in this upright position—then start running slowly. On your days for "form work" you may then accelerate for 50-150 meters, running as a lightly balanced puppet. Not only does the posture correct itself, but your chest is forward as are your hips—allowing for a quick touch-off with the feet. You may have to make little adjustments, but when you're lined up in a relaxed mode, running will be easier, and you'll feel less effort in the legs.

BOUNCE: Staying close to the ground

Upon watching the video replay, Tom was impressed with the way Sam's head stayed level as he ran. Tom, probably due to the strength in his legs from past training, had an inefficient tendency to push up in the air, to "lift off," which spent extra energy. Suzi and Sam didn't bounce, but appeared to have very little strength in their lower legs. They were advised to do hillwork p. 84 once a week, which would help to build up the calf muscle.

Strengthening the Push-off, with Hills

Hills will help anyone, but especially those that have less lower leg strength. See the Hill work section for more specific workouts. A basic hill workout is the following:

FIND A HILL: easy grade—so that you can run up without straining the muscles.

ACCELERATE: run harder than you normally run by increasing the turnover.

DON'T!: Do not lift the knees. Do not push off up into the air. Do not run all-out. Do not have a long stride.

LENGTH OF HILL: Beginners—50-100 yds./ Runners: 100-200 yards./ Competitors: 200-300 yds.

CONCEPT: Work on a quick push-off, with increased rhythm as you go up the hill. Keep a short stride. If the hill gets harder, shorten your stride. This builds strength and encourages you to turn over quicker at the same time.

Level!

The ideal clearance for the feet is minimal—just an inch or so off the ground. If your foot is close to the ground, your legs can go through a cycle faster—and you'll run faster. You won't spend excess energy pushing vertically up in the air. The energy you save will be available at the end of the run. The head stays relatively level.

CORRECTING BOUNCE—Keep those feet low to the ground

During your form-accelerations, avoid the temptation to lift off by taking a quick "touch-off" of the feet, staying low to the ground. On each successive acceleration, work on increasing turnover of the legs and feet, instead of the exuberant temptation to push the body up into the air.

The energy spent in excessive lift-off is mostly wasted. It causes two more problems: greater abuse on the foot upon landing and shock absorption; and 2) a need for the legs to go through some extraneous motion, during the extra time in the air. This is usually taken care of by a higher kick up behind the body, which will often cause the hamstring muscles to become more fatigued.

When in doubt, use less energy, stay lower to the ground, and turn over the legs quicker.

OVERSTRIDE:

As the forward leg absorbed body weight, a frame-by-frame analysis showed whether the lower leg made a 90-degree angle with the horizontal, or whether it was out in front of that position. Sam and Suzi were fine, while Tom had a tendency to overstride, especially when he ran at a faster pace.

CORRECTING OVERSTRIDE: Running easier

Our tendency to overstride is another attempt to counter slowing down with a quick-fix. Unfortunately, our intuitive sense of pace gets us into trouble in this area. As runners get tired, and realize that the main driving muscle are weakening due to fatigue, they subconsciously lengthen the stride to speed up. As in the case of other "quick fixes," this one will help for a short distance, but is very counterproductive later.

Longer strides will over-stretch the muscles, causing them to tighten up later, and weaken. If the stride is too long, it can put the knees or the muscles out of efficient mechanical range,

increasing recovery time and causing injury. Everybody has "weak links," places where they tend to get injured most often. When the main driving muscles are tired, the knees wobble more, and the "weak links" are likely to be pushed beyond their capacity. In other words, the damage will be greater.

When you feel tension in muscles which are at their limits—especially the calf and hamstring groups—you need to shorten the stride a bit more, to relax them. Keep shortening the stride until the leg muscles relax. This may allow you to pick up the turnover of the feet and legs. But even if this increase doesn't happen, you'll reduce the chance of injury, and speed up recovery due to the increased fatigue of overstriding. Often, the adjustment needed is a shortening of only an inch or two less than the overstride; but the relaxation it provides will allow the legs to go at a faster rhythm, so that some runners can actually speed up at the end of the race.

As you pick up the turnover on form accelerations, be sure to keep the stride short enough so that the leg muscles are relaxed and can maintain a quick rhythm. When in doubt, keep the stride short so that you can maintain a light, quick step on each of these pick-ups.

Lower Heart Rate—while running smoother and faster

While others in the group asked many questions about individual problems, Tom was still waiting for the heart monitor approach to form improvement. As the questions hit a lull, it was Tom's turn. The clinician took his heart rate monitor out of the box and started in.

"This is not just a counter of heart beats; it is one of the best bio-feedback devices ever devised to improve running form."

He went on to explain how, during hard workouts, most competitive athletes overtrain. The heart monitor tells you when you are in the target zone for improving anaerobic capacity.

When someone asked about the difference between aerobic and anaerobic, the clinician explained.

Aerobic Exercise is done at a comfort-able rate, so that the muscles will have an adequate supply of oxygen. The preferred fuel is fat, which produces a very small and manageable waste product, allowing the aerobic exerciser to continue until he or she reaches the endurance limit. The slower one goes, the longer this endurance limit can be pushed back.

Anaerobic Exercise pushes the muscles harder or further than they have been trained to go. In this over-exerted state, muscles must use stored sugar (glycogen), a fuel which produces a great amount of waste product. As the main waste, lactic acid, accumulates, muscles lose their capacity to do work. The faster one goes, the sooner he or she will reach the limit of exercise.

Afterward, Sam and Suzi joked about how the TV camera made them look dumpier and slower than they really were. Tom was unusually serious, and made no comments to Suzi about her dainty figure. While Sam and Suzi left for other activities, it suddenly hit Tom that there might be a variety of form improvements which could help him. He asked the clinician if there was a time when he could work with him. The teacher replied that the present was best, but that he needed to get some vegetables at Morrison's. Tom insisted that he buy. They talked specifics all the way down the mall, and Tom felt more involved in running than he had felt in years.

Galloway's Guerrilla Guide
Heart Monitors: Limiting workout damage by limiting the time above 80%

Your heart rate is an excellent indicator of the level of your exercise, provided that you don't dramatically extend the length of the workout beyond the level to which you're currently trained. When you're running below 70% of maximum heart rate, you are unlikely to over-train in intensity. (You can still overtrain by going farther than you've trained to go.) By keeping the heart rate between 70% and 80% of max heart rate, you can assume that your effort will normally produce a creative stress on the system, causing it to improve. This is the range you want to see during most of your speed workouts. But even the time spent in this 70%-80% range must be managed, so that you gradually increase.

But when you push the effort beyond 80% of max heart rate, you increase the recovery time of that workout. For those looking for top performance, incursions into the 80% and even occasional 90% bouts are fine (provided your doctor is fine with this). Because your recovery time and injury risk increase with the amount of time spent above 80%, the heart monitor can act as a damage control device.

Hard workouts like these should only be done once a week, and you should ease into the hard stuff. At first, make sure that you're only spending a few seconds at a time in the over-80% range. As the workouts progress, you can increase the length of the 80% plus a little, and also increase their frequency. Monitor your increase as follows: track the total number of minutes above 70%, above 80%, and above 90% in each speed workout, and don't let the increase in any segment of any one workout exceed 25% above that of the week before.

Remember that overwork can be cumulative: too many days per month of racing, speedwork, and long runs which are too fast (easy days should be run at least 2 minutes per mile slower than you could run that distance on that day).

Galloway's Guerilla Guide
Improving Form—and efficiency—by staying below 81%

The heart rate monitor is one of the best bio-feedback devices for improving form through efficiency. As always, the best environment for change is managed stress—and the monitor can tell you when to back off.

If you haven't been doing speedwork, once a week is as often as you should do this workout. Veteran speed trainers may do a second speed workout (or a race) during and leading up to racing season, but it should be less than the original. Again, be sure to monitor total workload, and recovery from races, speed, and long runs.

Distance: starts at the distance of an average run during the week.

Warmup: at least one mile of easy jogging, and one-half mile of accelerations (see "Putting It Together" chapter).

Venue: best at a track where you can monitor speed at a variety of short and longer intervals.

Workout:

Run repetitions of 800-1600 meters. Start each at (or slightly below) current race pace for the distance trained for. Increase intensity until you are at 70% of max heart rate until that feels natural and comfortable. Increase very gradually to 80% of max. Now you're ready for the workout. Your goal is to find form improvements that will allow you to run faster—yet stay at 80% of max heart rate (or below).

Techniques:

Shorten stride an inch or two and increase turnover of feet and legs.

Keep the push-off short and quick—and directly under the body.

Shift between different muscle groups as necessary—so that one group doesn't get tired.

Monitor: While you are monitoring your heart rate, time segments on the track of 200-400 meters at a time. When the distance of the repetition gets too long, (often after 800-1200 meters), your heart rate will increase. This is a sign for you to take a break: jog or walk for recovery and start again.

Warm-down: at least one mile of slow jogging and one-half mile of walking

Over turnip greens and rutabagas, Tom explained that several years ago, when he tried to run fast, he couldn't regain the smoothness of his youth. As they looked over the video another time or two, using a portable video unit, even Tom had to admit that he was overstriding when he ran fast, which caused him to have a forward lean at pushoff. The teacher, whose name was Trevor, explained the whole picture:

1. Yes, Tom reached too far forward on about every third stride. Trevor noted that his experience showed him that this tendency usually increased during the latter stages of races or hard workouts, causing the leg to stretch beyond its most efficient mechanical range. The extra touch of the foot, as he reached out, actually slowed him down, forcing him to push a little harder to speed up and maintain pace. Tom said that he noticed himself putting a little extra "reach" into his stride at the end of races and hard workouts, and felt that this helped speed him up. Trevor explained that this was only temporary, and often led to injury (most commonly the hamstring or the tendon band behind the knee) due to the lack of control in muscles fatigued from speed work or racing.

2. Tom pushed off a bit too hard, which wasted energy and fatigued the calf muscle more quickly. The extra distance off the ground forced the feet to endure more impact. This impact was partially absorbed by bending the knees excessively, (another inefficient motion).

3. The combination of overstriding, extra time in the air, and knee bending slowed down the turnover rate of the feet and legs. To make up for extra time in the air, the arms and shoulders went through a little extraneous motion, and the legs kicked up too far behind him. Trevor drew on the screen the various areas which caused the slowdown of Tom's rhythm, and estimated that he could pick up as much as 15 seconds a mile just on form improvements. This got Tom's attention.

When Tom mentioned that he was feeling an ache he had felt most of his running years (tightness in the hamstring), Trevor explained that even a slight overstride, of an inch or so, puts the leg and hamstring at a mechanical disadvantage. By reaching too far with our legs, we over-stretch the hamstring muscle, causing it to tighten up further,

Trouble-Shooting Your Form Problems

The Problem	The Cause	A Solution
Hamstring-Tightness	Overstriding	Shorten Stride
	High back kick	Upright posture & Less bounce
Tiredness in the lower back, neck or upper shoulders	Forward Lean	Upright posture
	Overstriding	Shorten Stride
Tightness in the calf muscles	Too much bounce	Run low to the ground
Tiredness or soreness in the Quads	Too much knee lift	Cut out knee lift—quick turnover (Low to the ground—less push-off)
Calf muscle fatigued	Too much bounce	Stay low to the ground
High back-kick	Forward Lean	Upright posture
Arm fatigue	Holding arms too far out & too much	Minimize arm motion Use "the paddle" arm motion
Tightness, pain, and early fatigue in the lower back and hips	Overstride	Shorten stride, work on turnover
Abnormal tiredness in the shoulders, arms and sometimes neck muscles	Arms held wrong or too much swing	Reduce arm swing, hold arms closer to body, paddle!

For more information on form and technique, see GALLOWAY'S BOOK ON RUNNING, *pp. 146-157.*

due to a condition called the stretch reflex. Tom was putting his hamstring through extra work by using it to lift the legs as they kicked up too high behind.

For more about the stretch reflex, see GALLOWAY'S BOOK ON RUNNING, p. 161.

Trevor asked Tom to do a few easy accelerations in the parking lot, telling him to work on staying light on his feet, with quick turnover. After 3 or four of these, Tom was looking very smooth on the flat. When he ran downhill, however, the oscillation came back. Tom was overstriding, and this forced his leg motion and shoulder rotation to be rough and jerky. After three or four more run-throughs, Tom found the correct combination of a slight shortening of the stride, lowered bounce and upright body posture. He was surprised that the refined form was easier.

Just to be sure, Trevor asked Tom to accelerate back and forth through an unused part of the parking lot for 15 or 20 more acceleration/glides. On the jog back, Trevor would make tiny adjustments, which Tom felt made him smoother and more efficient. On the last 3, Tom felt like he was floating—that the pavement was pushing him back up automatically. He felt great!

"I only shortened my stride about an inch, that's what it feels like. But that loosened up my hamstrings and made it easier to run faster. I feel lighter on my feet, like I'm barely touching the ground. The hardest thing for me to grasp is that I can run faster with less effort and tension."

"Maybe an old dog can learn a few new tricks."

or...becoming a smooth running machine

"**L**ast week's form session could have been called 'Tom's Tutorial,'" jabbed Suzi. Did you feel neglected this week, Tom?"

"Tom just needed more work than we did last week," laughed Sam. "He must have done his homework for today's session. He didn't even have to stay after school."

"If we're looking for those who can use more work, you might look at your arm swing, Suzi. You're not exactly paddling."

Suzi acknowledged that her shoulders rolled from side to side, but that she had tried to reduce the movement. Tom observed that Suzi was still exaggerating her arm motion, and still held her arms too far out from her body. Suzi acknowledged that she was often more tired in the arms and shoulders than in the legs and feet, especially when the course was hilly. But she confronted Tom. "What are you going to do about it?"

"Until he showed us the paddle, I still hadn't figured out what to do with the hands and arms." Suzi talked with a sly

The Paddle

One of the greatest challenges to a teacher of running form is that of reducing the flailing motion of the arms or hands. Even swinging the arms across the body will cause the upper torso to rotate from side to side—usually producing extra soreness or fatigue on long or hard sessions.

The Paddle is designed to keep your hands and arms where they should be—alongside the body. By absorbing the natural swinging motion with the lower arms and hands, the shoulders and upper arms can stay relaxed, and go along for the ride.

1. Drop your arms alongside the body. At first, just let them stay there, relaxed, by your side.

2. Start by letting the hands flop, according to the way they want to go—the motion will be the reciprocal of the motion of the feet. Keep your palms down, let the wrists bend as needed to let the hands flop alongside your shorts.

3. Let the lower arm (below the elbow) move also. Minimize the motion of the upper arm. This should allow the shoulders to stay relaxed and stable.

4. As the arms swing, try to keep the motion confined to that plane alongside the body—forward and back. Again, let the arms and hands relax—do not hold them in place or tighten the muscles. But try to avoid any swinging from side to side, particularly motion in front of the body which can causes body rotation.

The Push-off, or light touch-off

The ankle is the most important bio-mechanical construction which can aid running. When your body is lined up and the ankle moves into the right position, it will 'lift-off' almost automatically as the body moves forward, and the back leg gets into position.

1. Don't force the push-off, let it happen.

   You don't have to consciously push and use valuable energy. The most common result of pushing too hard is an extra bounce off the ground, which causes other problems.

2. A light touch of the foot.

   The ankle is programmed to respond quickly, with an efficient push forward. Because of the way your tendons are wrapped around the lever provided by your bone structure, you will receive this push with little or no cost in muscle energy. If you try to maximize the light touch of your feet, and don't force it, you'll receive a continuous flow of quick pushes throughout your run.

3. Forward motion. If you allow the ankle motion to be your main source of running motion, your movement will become more direct and forward. This helps to cut out extraneous motions of the foot and leg which will not just slow you down, but can lead to injury.

4. Your form accelerations will encourage a quick, efficient push-off, and will teach your ankle to become even more effective in controlling foot movements. Try to do these accelerations at least twice a week, every week.

5. Visualization helps! During any run, and particularly in the form accelerations, get a clear vision of your ankle moving through a very light quick yet effective forward push. Your vision includes the reduction and then the elimination of extraneous motion in the ankle area. As you work on this vision between accelerations, your form will improve.

smile on her face as she assumed the accent of a 'Valley girl.' "I can't stand messing up a great new, color-coordinated outfit with hands and arms that move in different directions."

"That Paddle technique helps me too," said Sam. "It takes the tension out of my shoulders—and there's lots to take out."

When Tom inquired about the latest on Sam's job situation, he heard the good news that while 25% of the professors had lost their jobs, Sam had been merely reassigned to the History Department. In order to accept the new position, Sam reported, the bad news was that he had to give up the rest of his 10-year research grant which had been shifted to a crony of the new president, to pad the crony's salary.

"How can that be? How can tenured professors be fired?" asked Tom.

"Their departments were eliminated—purely a technicality. Nobody knows what will happen next. And the resulting tension has made my exercise sessions so special. But while under this constant stress, the last thing I want to do is get out and exercise, and the only reason I do it is because I know you two will be here. I'm working on my 'belief environment,' but it just hasn't caught on yet."

Sam passed on another bit of good news. An editor from the *Journal of Anthropology* wanted to publish a status report of his research. It was giving him great satisfaction to tabulate his findings, which were more substantial than he thought."

Form Accelerations

1. Warm up with 5 minutes of slow walking, 5-10 minutes of faster walking, and then 5-10 minutes of slow running (with walking breaks, if desired).

2. Start each of the first 2-3 form accelerations with a slight downhill to give momentum. You'll only need 10-15 yards of slight downgrade to get your legs turning over a little faster than you usually run—and that's the speed you need for a form acceleration.

3. On each acceleration, work on the most efficient running form possible. See below for details. Generally this means having an upright body posture, running light on your feet which are low to the ground, and using a quick turnover of the feet.

4. After you have stabilized foot turnover on the flat for 50-100 yards, glide for 50-100 yards. Keep your feet low to the ground, stay smooth, and maintain the speed of the hill push, without expending much effort.

5. The gliding motion is very important for long term running enjoyment and for performance. You'll teach yourself how to use leg mechanics and momentum to "coast" at a fast pace. This allows you to shift away from the main driving muscles at regular intervals, so that they will have resiliency later in the run.

6. On the first acceleration, just use the momentum of the downhill start for propulsion. Then on each successive acceleration, you may increase the speed slightly by giving a small amount of energy to the forward push. This should feel natural. If it doesn't, then just glide through the acceleration, as on the first one.

7. Never sprint! You're trying to develop smooth and efficient form while increasing turnover. By trying to run all-out, you increase the chance of injury (and often learn some inefficient form lessons, such as over-striding). Keep the legs relaxed, and the leg muscles loose while you increase the turnover of legs and feet.

8. Beginners should start with accelerations which are only 50 yards or so, or about half a city block. If you've tried something like this before, you can increase the length to about 100 yards, about a full city block. Advanced speedworkers could run accelerations which are as long as 200 yards, mostly by gliding.

82

"Tom, I haven't called you back because I've been with patients all day! I couldn't even go out for lunch, it was PowerBar sandwich time."

"Look, Suzi, I know that physically I can do my workout this afternoon, but it's been a very bad day at the office. My son Chris doesn't want to

communicate, and I just don't feel motivated. Help!"

"Man, why today? I've been giving out "jump-start" word massages all day and could use some myself. You know, Tom, at shrink school they don't teach you any magic formulas, spells or give you pixie dust."

"I just want to know if you can help me get out

Galloway Guerrilla Guide
Why do we avoid doing something which we know will make us feel better?
How to pull the motivation deep from within—when it doesn't want to come

Causes of Low Motivation:

1. Low blood sugar, particularly at the end of the day. A performance snack such as PowerBar (with water, tea, or coffee) about one hour before exercise can help to get the blood sugar flowing.

2. Mental or physical scars from recent workouts when you've gone too hard, or too far. Through positive brainwashing techniques, you bypass this barrier by lowering the anticipated duress of the workout. (See Mind Power chapter)

3. Your left brain is in control. This center of negativity and excuses will work under any condition, but with particular power when you are under stress. First, get into a relaxed

mental mode where you feel in control (many go through relaxation techniques or meditate for a few minutes). Next, do something fun and positive. You can bypass or "wire yourself around" the left brain by going through a series of easy steps which gradually lead to the workout. The more you have mentally rehearsed this, the easier it gets. If you can get under the control of the right brain, you'll have better success. (See "Mindpower" chapter).

4. At first, the workout isn't fun. Keep searching for parts of it which can spark your interest, or make it come alive, such as special places, special music, friends, a new outfit, a different energy drink, etc.

5. Reinforce yourself at each step of the way. When you keep going during a tough part, congratulate yourself. Reward yourself with a drink of water or sport drink, or a strategic walking break.

the door today, OK?"

Suzi thought for a few seconds and then shifted mental gears. "OK, I'll fax you a motivation sheet from the Galloway Guerrilla Guide and then we can talk. It'll take me 30 minutes to get it together so grab a cup of coffee and a PowerBar in the meantime."

About 45 minutes later as Tom was leaving, the phone rang. He started to leave, but looked back at the phone. Then, just before the answering machine picked up his call, he grabbed it. "Hey Sam, oh no, you can't sneak out on us. Look, I wasn't going to do the workout either, it's so dreary. But I'll fax you the 'inspiration sheet' which Suzi sent. And I hate to admit it but one PowerBar and a cup and a half of coffee has me on my way. We're going to run the hill behind the amphitheater at Chastain Park. I'm going to be very disappointed in you if you don't show up. See you there."

Tom had all of his clothes with him, but pulled into the Phidippides parking lot for a pair of socks anyway. Just listening to the exchange of positive ideas among staff and customers perked him up mentally, and started the focus toward his workout. As he drove toward Chastain Park, he played a Bob Dylan cassette (Greatest Hits II) which he had used before workouts in the 70's to get mentally ready. He could never explain why this music did the job, it just did. By the time he had parked along the street in front of the Chastain golf shack he was feeling very positive—but pulled out his final motivational trump card—a special pair of racing flats. The glove fit

Galloway's Guerrilla Guide
Out the Door Boosters

1. A blood sugar insertion—coffee, PowerBar, etc.
   Your blood is ready to flow, and the energy is ready to rise, you just need something to get it started.

2. Visit to Phidippides, health club, etc.
   There is a chemical effect when personalities interact. Positive energy inspires the positive part of any person's personality.

3. Music
   Keep around several tapes which get you "fired up." Keep some at home, some at work, and some with you in your briefcase, purse, etc. "Your" music will help you connect with other positive experiences which you've associated with the same music.

4. A series of inspirational quotes.
   Keep them taped to your briefcase, in your purse, on your desk, so that you can read them regularly. When you find a good one, add it to the list.

5. A special pair of shoes—shorts, shirt, hat
   Never underestimate the power of rewards. When you accomplish something, no matter how small, give yourself a reward. As you make more progress, reward yourself with clothing and shoes. In this way, you are associating successful experiences with the clothing. As you put on the clothing, you can visualize the past successful experiences.

of this shoe brought back the confidence of races in which he had run well. When he saw Sam and Suzi arrive, he had forgotten why he had not been motivated earlier.

As the coffee was brewing, Sam went into his living room for 3 minutes of silence and meditation. After putting a bit of cinnamon, sugar, and coffee into his car-cup, he hit the road to the melody of his favorite classical music. The music seemed to permeate his brain, bringing thoughts of inspirational quotes from Winston Churchill, and others, which motivated him.

Suzi had already been going through the steps of the "out the door" boosters she had faxed to Tom and Sam, but knew that she needed a little extra push for herself. It was time for the unveiling of the flashy new outfit she had given herself as a reward for completing the last long workout without whining. It worked; she relived the success of that day and was ready to face the fitness world.

All were in good spirits as they started together, but Suzi noticed that Tom looked more like an athlete than she had noticed before. Maybe it was the racing shoes, and the improved bio-mechanics which they promoted. But when she looked more closely at his face, she didn't see as much of the double chin. She dearly loved to "kid" him about his weight.

"Tom, I hate, with all of my being, to admit this, but you've lost weight," she remarked.

"Ten pounds, and my running feels better for it!" admitted Tom. "I've been pretty regular with my three work-week jogs. It started when I called Chris, offering to go for a run. He told me over the phone how his memory of me is from some old running pictures, when I was 30 pounds lighter. When he put off the run until next week, it gave me time to get in a bit of shape before he saw me, but I did warn him of my extra 'blanket.'"

"Isn't it hard," asked Suzi, "to run with us, now that you're getting into better shape?"

"I used to think that running slowly was harder on my body than running faster," agreed Tom. "I now know that this was an ego thing. But just because I realize that, doesn't mean that I can control myself all the time." They ran and walked along West Wieuca before turning up Pool Road, beside the old Chastain Park swimming pool. Sam started struggling badly, even while walking, as they reached the steep hill beside the amphitheater. They began walking more slowly and Tom admitted that on a hill that steep, his muscles were getting a better warm-up by walking instead of risking overexertion by running up.

On the other side of the amphitheater, Sam and Suzi walked and watched as Tom did 2 accelerations in the parking lot on the upper level. Tom walked with them between each. Suzi nudged Sam to try some of these at their own speed. They practiced short strides, quicker turnover and got into the groove after 4. Tom had to slow Suzi down on the third one. She was trying to prance like a well-bred horse.

After the first one Tom felt "rough" so he slowed down the second one, working on being smooth. He started out slow on the next, but the muscles warmed up and he speeded up without putting out any more effort. Tom admitted that the slight downhill grade gave him a push, and he was enjoying gliding through the rest of the parking lot. On the last two he didn't feel like he was 20 years old, but was running as smoothly. Several times he started to lengthen his stride and made an immediate correction. Suzi told Tom that he seemed to be gliding at the

end. Sam actually timed Tom on each and noted that his times were faster at the end of the acceleration. Tom was surprised to hear this, because the last ones felt almost effortless.

As Tom moved to the hill behind the amphitheater for his workout, Sam and Suzi walked and jogged up the hill. They used the "huff & puff" gauge to guide their exertion. When they started

GGG
The Hill Workout

Hill Grade: Gentle

Distance:
Beginning runners—50-100 meters
Runners who are starting hill work—100-200 meters
Speedwork, or hillwork veterans—200-300 meters

Warmup:
Walk 5 minutes
Jog slowly 5-10 minutes
Jog at comfortable pace 5-10 minutes
Walk for 3-4 minutes

Accelerations:
Try to use a slight downhill to get the momentum, and legs, moving smoothly.
Shorten stride, increase turnover, keeping leg muscles loose and relaxed.
Pick up momentum for the first third of the acceleration, then coast.
During the coasting, glide with the same rhythm while decreasing the effort.
Walk 1 minute between accelerations, and/or jog very slowly for 1 minute.
Walk 3-4 minutes between accelerations and the hill work. Remember: Don't sprint

Hills:
If possible, get a gentle downhill boost of 20-30 meters—to give you momentum going up.
Keep a short stride, and shorten further if the incline of the hill increases.
Run the first one slow, increase slightly on the second one, and get into the workout on the third.
Run the first one about 10K race pace, the second about 5K race pace.
The other hills should be run at most a bit faster than 5K race pace, but never all-out.
Make sure that the leg muscles feel relaxed and loose while the legs turnover faster.
Walk down the hill for complete recovery.
If your legs are cramping or tightening up, try shortening your stride. If that doesn't work, run slower on the hills. If the legs still don't feel right, warm down and stop the hard part of the workout.

Warmdown:
Jog slowly for 5-10 minutes
Walk for 5-10 minutes

For more information on hill work, see GALLOWAY'S BOOK ON RUNNING, pgs. 57, 170 to breathe heavily, they walked. While Tom did 6 hills, they did 4—at their own speed--and felt comfortable. On a 200-yard hill, they usually jogged 3 segments of 40 yards each and walked two segments of about 40 yards each.

Tom started to feel tension in his hamstrings on the second hill, and realized that he was extending his foot out in front of him a bit too much. He shortened it and was able to almost instantly speed up the turnover of his feet and legs. By the end of the workout he was feeling smoother with a short quick stride—and running faster—than he had with the long stride on his first ones.

But on the last hill, Tom's instincts from his earlier macho days were just too strong. When fatigue started to slow him down, Tom took off with a powerful stride. While very tired, Tom was gratified to feel a surge of power, and he continued to go quickly down the other side of the hill. He would have liked to have taken this back, but it was too late. Suzi noticed that Tom had restrained himself during most of the workout, keeping the stride under control. Tom explained that the lessons he learned at the Phidippides form clinic hadn't fully clicked in until he saw the coverage of the Boston Marathon the previous Monday.

"I turned it on at the half way point with Germany's Uta Pippig on the screen. I had never seen her and thought she was jogging. Her stride was so short and her turnover so smooth that she looked slow, but she was winning the race. Her closest competition, Elena Meyer from South Africa, had great form, with a strong push-off, and good knee lift. I had to keep looking because the contrast in styles was so dramatic.

"Then I realized that this was a classic example of what Trevor at Phidippides had been saying. If you save your main driving muscles by maintaining a cruising motion, you'll conserve resources needed at the end. As Elena cramped up near the end—probably due to the excess strength of her powerful stride—Uta just jogged along and ran 2:25! That's faster than I ran in my competitive career."

As the trio did their slow warm-down, Tom kept coming back to how strong he felt. "Today I felt like I did when I was 25 and that was the last time I beat Dylan."

"You sure looked frisky today, especially on the last one," said Suzi. "But why don't you wait and see how you feel tomorrow?"

Each was in for a surprise the following morning.

Tom knew some thing was wrong when he stood up out of bed. He expected soreness and tightness as he moved toward the bathroom, but something wasn't working right. He put on a pair of warm-up pants and a t shirt, and tried to do some stretching exercises, hoping that some additional flexibility would make it feel better but no luck.

After 2 rings, Suzi caught Tom's call. "You too? I feel like the dregs this morning. Yeah, the same with me. I hobbled to the dresser and wondered what have I done to myself. So what did Sam say about his legs. Yeah, my pain is similar, if we're lucky it's just the

Galloway's Guerrilla Guide
How to treat it—if I think it's an injury

- Ice—rub a chunk of ice on the injured area until the surface is numb (about 10 minutes)
- Don't stretch any muscles or tendons in the general area of the injury
  (the only exception might be the I-T band on the outside of the knee. Ask your doc!)
- Take at least 2-3 days off running (and stay away from other exercise which uses the same area)
- Start an alternative exercise program, if you even guess that you'll be off for more than 3 days. The best alternative exercises for running are water running and cross country skiing machines.

(for more information on treating specific injuries, see GALLOWAY'S BOOK ON RUNNING, pp. 199-227.)

How to tell if it's an injury:

- inflammation (swelling)
  external swelling is easy to spot—
  internal swelling is harder to spot— but leaves the entire area larger
- loss of function
- significant pain that doesn't go away—or increases

(For more info on injuries, see GALLOWAY'S BOOK ON RUNNING, pp. 198-225).

normal round of aches and pains. I'll send you a handout on how to tell if it's an injury. You're to blame, you got us all inspired and we over-did it!"

(2 hours later) "Suzi, that sound in the background is my upper calf muscle screaming. Seriously, this is not going away. What should I do? Is there anything in your GGG about this? I didn't realize it before this happened, but I'm starting to get hooked on the

running again, and I want to get this injury behind me. If I can't get some help soon, I may have to sign on as one of your clients. Call back soon."

"Sorry I didn't get back to you sooner, lots of problems today. I've just faxed over some GGG sheets on injury, but if you have a question, just call the folks at Phidippides, they've not only gone through this a thousand times themselves, they get feedback from thousands of customers. Come to think of it, they do such a good job of listening to addicted-but-injured runners that they probably take business away from me and my profession. I should complain!"

"Suzi, the pain is no better today, and the calf muscle won't even work right when walking. I've got an appointment with an orthopedist. No, a podiatrist who specializes in the foot and injuries which are caused by the action of the foot. Well, one example would be a knee problem caused by the turning in of the foot at push-off, I think it's called over-pronation. Since this is primarily a leg injury, I'll stick with an orthopedist."

"Well, Tom, Sam and I are going to walk today and see how it goes. Both he and I don't notice any swelling, and the muscles seem to work OK, they just rebel every time we try them out. I guess we'll see how bad things are around the Piedmont Park loop."

(The next day) "Hey Tom, it's the hypochondriac watch. How's YOUR ache or pain today?" asked Suzi.

"Dr. G. was very thorough and said that it was a minor pull of the calf muscle. She didn't prescribe anything, but said that my cast-iron stomach could probably handle Advil—2 tablets every 4 hours, with a meal or a "significant snack" each time. I'm supposed to drink lots of water all day. She also suggested massage. No! from a massage therapist who specializes in runners. I've already gotten a couple of recommendations from running central, Phidippides. She mentioned running in the water. Don't you have a GGG handout on that?"

Tom and Sam arrived at the Buckhead YMCA at the same time. As they walked to the locker room, Sam showed off his water running belt which the Phidippides folks had found to be the best for doing water running workouts. "I never have felt comfortable in the water," said Sam. This is supposed to give a secure feeling, and help to put me into position to run correctly in the water."

"Speaking about that," said Tom, "I hope that Suzi is here to show us how to do this. The handout was pretty good, but it really helps to have the information given directly. So tell me, Sam, you have an achilles injury?"

"Yes Tom, my foot didn't work quite right when Suzi and I walked around the park. We stopped by Phidippides to pick up a cryo-cup to ice it at home, and they were having one of the "dollar doctor" clinics. The podiatrist took a look at my foot for the sum total of $1 and said that I had a slight strain of the achilles, which was common when doing more hills than I'm used to doing. He was kind enough to not mention the effect of the extra poundage which I'm carrying around."

"I guess he told you to do lots of stretching?"

"No. He said that most injuries will be prolonged if you stretch them while injured. Just as the healing starts, a good stretch will tear it up again. He's seen dozens of runners who have doubled or tripled their recovery time by stretching the injured area.

"You know, that makes sense. I wish I had known that 10 years ago when I tried to stretch my way out of an achilles injury myself, and it lasted over 3 months! One of the tragedies of youth is that during that physically resilient time, we are able to abuse our limits—and still recover fairly fast."

"Unfortunately," noted Sam "when the damage is structural as in contact sports, there is great suffering and loss of function later in life. I have some lasting damage in the ankle and heel from my short high school football career, which may be aggravating this achilles injury."

Suzi was waiting for them at the pool and had a corner of the deep end designated as the "water racing zone". She shivered as they got into the water, and started showing them the motion—to keep warm.

"You may not realize it as you're running, but the front leg kicks out, then comes through a range of motion in which the leg goes behind you."
Tom had the motion pretty well down, but kicked too far out in front. Sam reduced his motion to that of cycling. "This is too easy," he said.

Suzi told him that he was right, moving his lower legs in a small circle. This produced very little resistance, and therefore, very little effort was required. Unfortunately, it didn't give a significant workout. Suzi showed him how to kick out and pull through. He noticed the difference immediately, in terms of increased resistance and more effort.

The first day, Suzi let them water-run for 5 minutes, take a 5 minute break, and then another 5 minutes. Afterward, Sam tried swimming with his head out of water, and could only do it for one lap of the pool. When Tom asked him why he swam that way, Sam explained that he learned that way, because he was afraid of the water. Suzi mentioned that swimming with head raised on a regular basis builds up the upper shoulders and back better than regular swimming.

"You were just ahead of your time and didn't know it," commented Tom.

"I hate to bring this up—just when we've been having so much fun—but why are we doing this?" asked Tom.

Suzi, looking a bit irritated, said that she was surprised that he was so far out of it, that Dylan had been doing these run-water workouts for 2 years. There was one stretch last summer when he developed an injury every week and did more running in the pool than on dry land.

What did he think he was getting out of it?" asked Tom.

Suzi said that the GGG listed 3 major benefits: improved running form, stronger running "back-up" muscles, all in the venue of a cardiovascular "sanity" session for the head without pounding.

"Come to think about it, Dylan's form was much more smooth after the water workouts than I remember it."

"The resistence of the water forces the legs to find the most efficient motion. Dylan had several little extraneous motions which Galloway found on video tape, and which he virtually eliminated after two and a half months in the water. Dylan also felt that it strengthened some alternative muscle groups which could back up the main driving groups when they were fatigued.

This fits into Galloway's idea about team-work of muscle groups. If you allow the various groups to rest early and often, you'll get a higher level of performance out of all of them at the end because they are more resilient.

Suzi agreed—to the point of almost having to pull the two out of the pool. "It's like any new form of exercise—if you do too much of it too soon, you'll over-fatigue the muscles. Take it easy.

Before they left, Suzi showed Sam and Tom three different pool running motions.

When Sam asked how much bouncing back and forth should be done between the various water running "strides", Suzi said that most runners seemed to use the basic motion most of the time. The Sprint is used primarily by injured runners who wanted to retain some capability in running faster (both form and anaerobic capacity). The Cross Country Ski motion is done in bursts

and bestows leg strength as it adds variety to the workout.

The trio adjourned to the exercise room and played for a few minutes at a time on the exercise cycle, the rower, and other machines before Suzi became the enforcer again. When Tom became a little "macho" on the stair machine, she explained that he was probably using

Your Basic Distance Stride

Run as you would on land, keeping the legs and feet in an efficient and smooth motion. The knees bend naturally as your leg swings forward and your leg almost straightens out as it goes through what would be the push-off phase on dry land.

Cross Country Ski

With almost straight legs(little bend at the knees) move the legs like sissors through the water. This strengthens the hips, butt muscles, and lower back. At first go through a moderate range of motion. For increased strength building, increase the range of motion, but only a few strides at first. Over the months you may increase the frequency or the extent of this motion as desired. Usually, this motion is inserted into the "basic" stride in 20-60 second intervals.

The Sprint

With your feet directly underneath you, shorten the basic running motion and do it very quickly. This will get the heart rate up, and will increase respiration. You know you're doing this right if your head pops out of the water more than before. You should also move the arms in the running motion which will give the shoulders a workout also.

Note 1. Don't let your legs get out of the range of motion for your current capabilities. The resistence of the water can over-extend muscles which are not ready for the motion.

Note 2. Check with your doctor, physical therapist, etc before doing the water running, if injured. There are very few injuries which could be aggravated by this activity, and it's always best to check.

Warning about Stair Machines

- Many of the motions used during a stair machine workout use running muscles

- Don't use stair machines if any of these muscles are injured.

- Stair machines build strength in the same way as hill work.

- Can be used as a second workout on a running day.

- Shouldn't be done as an alternataive on a non-running day—because the muscles don't recover.

muscles that needed rest. Tom agreed that he was violating the first rule of cross training for injury—use muscles which are not injured.

"I gotta tell you guys, you're going to get sore if you work the muscles too hard in the first workout," she warned, with a tone of guilt.

"You would spoil it—just as we're learning how to have fun—being macho," criticized Tom.

Sam & Tom's Cross Training/Water Running Program

Mon	Tue	Wed	Thu	Fri	Sat	Sun
Week I						
Walk 30 min	5-7 min H2O twice 10 min of XT	Walk 30min	7-9 min H2O twice 15 min of XT	off	10-12 H2O twice 15 min XT	walk 60min
Week II						
10 min H2O twice 20 min XT	walk 30min	12min H2O twice 20 min XT	walk 30min	12 min H2O twice 25 min XT	off	35 min H2O 15min XT
Week III						
walk 30 min 20 min XT	15 min H2O run/walk 1mi	walk 30 min 20 min XT	15 min H2O run/walk 2mi	off	15 min H2O run/walk 3 mi	walk 20 min XT
Week IV						
10 min H2O 3-5 mi run	walk 30min XT	10 min H2O 4-6mi run	walk 30 min XT	10 min H2O 4-6 mi run	off	long run

Note: XT means alternating between swimming, rowing, nordic track, and weights (it's best not to stop, moving from one activity to the next)

93

Tom couldn't believe that he was in such pain. As the massage therapist moved her trained hands up and down his calf muscle, she quickly found the injured area. After more warm-up massage to the lower leg, she started working on the damaged area itself. Tom waited for a while to say it but finally had to overcome his macho instincts:

"Should I tell you if it hurts. Really bad?"

When the therapist nodded in the affirmative, Tom immediately told her that she was producing more pain than he had ever experienced in his life. She thanked him for breaking it to her gently and that he could be more direct next time."

She explained that he had pulled one of the components of his calf muscle, and guessed that he had been running up and down hills. She had worked on lots of runners, and that's why she had been recommended so highly by Phidippides. Tom was impressed with her ability to read the subtlities of the muscle and the damage. But he was also impressed how a gentle and fragile looking woman could produce such pressure and pain during the treatment.

Tom was concerned that she was pushing too hard and setting back the healing process. She said that she had become very sensitive to the danger of aggravating the injury, but that it was his choice. If she worked hard and painful, it might take 3-4 treatments to work out the problem. But she could work easier and have it take as many as 10-12 treatments. As Tom calculated her fees he said that would be willing to deal with the pain, he thought."

The Benefits of Massage

- To promote blood flow into an injured area.

- To break up and move the "junk" out of the injured area (which interferes with the healing process.)

- To encourage a faster regeneration of the injured area through manipulation and tissue work.

On Selecting a Massage Therapist

1. Muscle injuries usually respond best to massage. Effective treatments with an therapist who knows running and the injured area can speed up healing and minimize the chance of the injury coming back. Ask your running friends, running stores, running clubs, and other running contacts for the best and most experienced massage therapists, and start your selection process.

2. It helps to have someone who has been recommended by several runners, particularly those who've had the same problem you're experiencing. It's OK to ask the therapist to supply you with a list of clients who have been "massaged through" the same injury you're experiencing.

3. You will have to rely upon the therapist for making many judgement calls. Therefore judgement and experience are primary components in your choice of the best candidate.

Massage and the Healing Process

1. An injured area(muscle, tendon, etc) has "junk" around it. These substances have been brought in during injury and repair. Unfortunately, the alien substances often slow down the healing process. In other cases they will allow the healing to proceed—but not to be completed.

2. Massage helps to break up the "junk" and move it out of the area.

3. The increased blood flow, which is encouraged by massage, will also speed your recovery.

Tom asked if there was a time period after the injury that was a "no-massage zone." She told him that the healing should have started. "To massage an injured area too soon can slow down the healing process."

A bit concerned, Tom asked, "how can you tell whether the injury can handle it or not. "

"Oh, I can tell. There's a certain level of inflamation and damage which leaves the muscle feeling "nebulous," with no integrity of form, or response. If I find any of that on your injury, I'll back off, or stop."

After the first session, Tom limped out of the office, and felt the injury more than he had felt since it actually happened. He was sure that the therapist must have done something wrong. But when he woke up the following morning, it was noticeably better. The morning after the third session, Tom went for a run—and felt healed.

Just for insurance, he went for one more session after the injury pain was gone.

TO LOOK LIKE AN ATHLETE

As they walked by theY's weight room, Tom stopped to see why a crowd had gathered and he noticed a flyer on the wall promoting a clinic being conducted by Jeff Galloway on "postural muscle strengthening exercises." Sam found a place for both of them in the back of the crowd.

than that of an "average endurance wimp."

It was an ironic scene—a crowd of generally muscled people being taught about strength exercise by a skinny fellow. After going through the lesson—which only took about 5 minutes, the crowd, became surprisingly curious, and the questions began.

It was evident that most of the attendees were regular users of the equipment in the room. Jeff started with the statement that his presentation would take no more than 10 minutes and that anyone who wanted to use the equipment could do so while he was talking. Several "jocks" took him up on that. Sam and Tom looked around at the many muscle-bound folks and agreed that the two of them were beyond hope, unless Gallo-way had some miracle program. Suzi, who had just joined them, whispered that there were some miracle pills but that the side effects were not very promising. When Sam got a good look at Galloway for the first time he chuckled and said that he wouldn't expect many muscle development ideas to come out of a fellow like that. Suzi said that Galloway had described his muscle development as only marginally better

As Sam and Tom walked into the swimming area, they were laughing about something that had occurred in the locker room, Suzi was waiting for them, somewhat annoyed that "the boys" had some joke that they were keeping from her. As they got into the pool for an easy warm up of the water running motion, Tom let her in on the locker room chat.

"After Galloway's talk, there were two muscle jocks who weren't buying the fact that you could get so much benefit in 5-10 minutes. They tried to poke a hole in the concept, but failed. So after Galloway left the room one of the muscle guys said 'I just realized what it is about that program that I really couldn't get into. I don't want to look like Jeff Galloway'."

Galloway's Postural Muscle Program

Note: before trying any of these exercises, talk to a muscle training expert to design a strength training program that will work for you, avoid structural problems, and compensate for special weaknesses. The muscle exercises listed below are only used as examples and are not to be a specific program for anyone, unless recommended by a muscle training expert. As in any training program, ease into exercises by only doing one easy trial the first day, followed by two easy ones the second day, and so forth. After 5 or 6 regular sessions, don't do the program more often than every other day.

Purpose: To strengthen muscle groups which help to maintain upright posture, and the efficiency of breathing.

Time Required: 5-10 minutes, once or twice a week

Target Muscle Groups: neck, shoulders, upper back, lower back, and stomach.

Stomach: bent knee sit-up

There are two positions for this exercise, both performed in the "crunch" position (lie on your back, bend knees, and barely raise your head and neck off the floor. Go through a small range of motion which keeps the muscles contracted continuously. This strengthens the upper abdominal group from approximately the navel to the beginning of the pectoral, or chest group. The second position is assumed by raising your head, neck and shoulders a bit more off the floor and working on the lower abs below the navel. Again, work through a very narrow range of motion, keeping the muscles contracted throughout the exercise.

Lower Back: the back curl

Lie on your stomach on a padded bench. Hook your feet underneath as an anchor, moving your upper body—above the navel—off the end. Let your head go down near the floor, raising your trunk so that it is even with the level of the bench, then repeat. (Again, get the advice of a muscle expert before doing this or any exercise.)

Upper Back and Shoulders: upright rowing

Use dumbells, bar bells even home-made weights such as gallon jugs with water. Stand upright, and lift the weights in each hand maintaining an upright body posture up to chest level, and then lower slowly. Your elbows are held out to the side of the body and should be held higher than the hands.

Neck and Upper Shoulder: shoulder shrug

With weights in each hand, keep your arms at your side and lift your shoulders gently up and down.

The Upper Running Body—As A Whole: the running motion with dumbells

Pick a light dumbell in each hand and swing your arms as you should in running. You may lift the weight a bit higher than you actually do, when you run and can also let it swing a bit further back. Always keep the hands swinging in a plane alongside the body.

97

Tom was about to leave his house early when the phone rang. He started to walk out, but something told him that he should answer, so he raced over before the answer machine clicked on.

"Hi, Chris""Yea, today is still OK. Yea, meet at the Peachtree finish line. See you there."

kidded Tom about his obvious nervousness in seeing his son for the first time in 3 years. As they pulled up in front of the Galloway School, Sam got in and Suzi said "let's run here." The view overlooking the golf course was inviting, with rolling green hills and expanses of open fairways. This time Tom became the DI. "No, we're going to learn the Peachtree course," he said, "and besides, Suzi, we parked your car near the finish line. So if you want to retreive it you'll have to earn it back."

As Tom's 10 year old Honda Civic turned right onto Roswell Road and headed North, Suzi barked out her orders like a drill sargent "get in the left lane and turn left." Tom obeyed and sighting a break in the Southbound lane accelerated into a hard left which sent Suzi sliding into the rattletrap door, which sounded like it might give way under the pressure.

"It's OK," said Tom, "nobody's gotten killed on any of my turns like that—to my knowledge."

"Well, remind me to ride Marta next time—or hitchhike." countered Suzi.

As they headed North on Powers Ferry Rd the Chastain Park golf course was beautifully clothed in its green blanket, with white sprinkles of dogwood. Suzi

Tom glanced back at the large white columns of the main building of the school as they pulled away and asked "so what makes this school different?"

"Being an educator, I'm probably a bit too meticulous in choosing a school for my children. There are several schools in town which offer as good a primary and secondary education as you can get anywhere, but this school encourages and rewards a positive attitude about learning. The graduates here come away with the best education and the self-esteem to put it to work.

Suzi explained that she had met the

founder, Elliott Galloway, Jeff's father, at the fitness vacation the previous summer. She was impressed that at age 74, Elliott still ran about as many miles per week as the son, and often ran a marathon or two per year. Suzi also found very interesting his philosophy of education and asked Sam how it actually worked in the real world of kids, discipline, and achievement tests.

Sam told how each child develops responsibility for his or her learning. A low ratio of students to committed teachers encourages each child to develop at his or her own level in each subject. Tom said it sounded like one of those "California ideas" of the 60's. Sam explained it has been one of the shining examples of how kids can learn to enjoy learning while achieving at the highest academic levels. Schools from all over the country send observers who say that this is the direction education must head. "The achievement tests show that my kids are learning above grade level in everything and they have never said that they didn't want to go to school."

At this point, they pulled into the parking lot at Lenox Square Mall and Tom explained that on July 4th they should take Marta and walk up to the main parking lot along Peachtree Rd.

Sam admitted that he was getting nervous even though this was only a training session. Tom told him that it is natural to feel that way before a challenge. They walked along Lenox Road to Peachtree, as Suzi bragged about how she was resisting the pull of the giant magnet which normally forced her— against her will—into Lenox Mall. Tom

suggested that she imagine that the giant magnet be placed at the finish line of Peachtree.

"That won't work," said Suzi, "there are no shops there"

On the previous Sunday, they had covered 5 miles using liberal walking breaks. Tom felt that it was time to get to know the course. This was the long run which Sam and Suzi had looked forward to, and dreaded, at the same time. They would do this tour three times. The first tour was designed only as a completion exercise only.

At the intersection of Lenox and Peachtree Roads, they paused. Tom pointed North on Peachtree with his right hand and said that on race day they would be walking about 800-1000 yards or more in that direction before lining up. They turned left on Peachtree and walked to the main entrance of Lenox Mall: the official start of the Peachtree Road Race.

As they jogged for two minutes and walked for two minutes, Tom described how the elite athletes gather in that area before the race for last minute warm-up and stretching. Suzi and Sam listened to Tom, and felt the tension and excitement of these "race horses" getting ready to go out of the gate. The flat first mile of the course was great for sight-seeing, Tom recommended. It went right through Buckhead, one of Atlanta's premier business districts. Atlanta's only toll road, GA 400 tunnelled underneath them and under a major financial center. Sam pointed ahead and said that he had his investments of at least $2.25 in the

Robinson Humphrey brokerage in that building. Tom said that the stock market went up yesterday. It might be worth $2.30 today!

After the first mile, Tom said they were in for a treat. Suzi asked where would they stop for frozen yogurt, etc. Tom meant that the Peachtree course turns to the left in the center of the Buckhead district and starts down a wonderfully gentle downhill for 1.5 mi. As they passed the intersection of Peachtree and Paces Ferry Rds, Tom noted that this was the start of the first Peachtree Road Race. Pointing to the block on the right, he explained how the original director, Tim Singleton, opened up the trunk of his car, in the parking lot of what was the Buckhead Sears at the time. Entries were taken on the spot, and 110 folks were off for "Five Points" and the center of downtown Atlanta.

Both Suzi and Sam asked Tom for any tidbits from the first year, when he was 17 years old.

"What was running like, back then," asked Sam, who was huffing and puffing less on this gentle down hill, and enjoyed the chance to talk on the two minute walking breaks.

You knew most of the folks in the race—mostly young competitors in high school, college or those who had just graduated. The "old timers," in their 30's, stood out because there were so few of them.

Suzi had to hold herself on the road again as she passed her favorite coffee place, Starbucks. The next mile had

even more downgrade, and some beautiful scenery. They passed St. Phillips which looked like european cathedral, followed by several of the city's most prominent churches including Second Ponce de Leon Baptist, and Christ the King. Sam had to force himself to hold back on some of the downhill running 2 minutes. Suzi had no trouble keeping on pace, but found it so easy that she was tempted to run through the walking breaks. On this day, Tom became the voice of conscience.

"The hot blast of reality is near. We're going to pull a long hill right after we bottom out at Peachtree Creek, about 2.5 miles into the race."

This was enough to get the attention of his teammates. They took every walking break and enjoyed the wide, tree-lined street with glimpses of the downtown skyline. Suzi showed them the high-rise where Elton John was reported to live. They played some more until noticing the low point of the entire course, the Peachtree Creek bridge.

They hadn't noticed how shady it had been going downhill, until the uphill started and the sun seemed to heat up a notch. Tom noted that they were burning more fuel going up hill and generating more body heat. But Sam and Suzi got the full effect of the sun, the hill, and the effort as sweat beads poured off. At first, the uphill energized the leg muscles in a different way, and felt good. Suzi felt too good and pushed a bit too hard. The hill seemed to level off, so she speeded up to "get it over with." Only 300 yds further, where the grade increased toward Piedmont Hospital,

Suzi begged for an extra minute on the walking break. As they passed the Piedmont Health and Fitness Club where Sam worked out, he admitted that he was under control with the walking breaks of 3 minutes, after 2 minutes of running. Suzi had to walk all of the last 100 meters of the hill.

At the top they took a long walk break and sweated, Suzi wanted to sit down, but Tom wouldn't let her. After 5 minutes of sweating and panting, Suzi said that she was ready to jog for a minute. Tom asked her several questions to see if she was showing the signs of heat disease.

The Warning Signs of Heat Disease

Extreme Heat Build-Up in the Face and Head

Hot and Cold Flashes

Cessation of Sweating

Clammy Skin

Inability to Concentrate—or realize where you are

The flat terrain and some shade helped Suzi come around. "I thought seriously about telling you guys to go ahead, but I'm feeling better now." she said. Tom blamed himself for not holding Suzi back during the first part of the hill. They continued the two minute jog and three minute walk, crossing over Interstate 85, up a gradual mile-long hill past WSB's White Columns, and past the High Museum of Art. Suzi looked for, and found, many interesting things to keep her stimulated—small specialty shops, outdoor cafes, other runners, lots of walkers, and some dogs who were taking their humans crested long this incline at Colony Square, Suzi was tired but under control. She told the group to go back to 2 minutes of walking and two of jogging. Sam started to really open up, letting his thoughts fly.

"That Piedmont Hospital hill was a real milestone for me. While I'm tired and perspiring, I'm also a bit exhilarated. I can really see how those beginners in the Galloway marathon program are able to start from no endurance and finish a marathon in 6 months; and what a feeling of accomplishment! This also sheds an interesting light on my study of mass migrations of ancient peoples. If my sedentary, unhealthy body can drag along at 15 minutes per mile, and that 50 year-old woman I met at Piedmont Hospital Classic could cover 26 miles in 5 hours, then a hardened ancient migrator should have been able to trek along at 15 minutes per mile, almost indefinitely. This opens up the possibilities for much faster migrations than I could have believed.

Sam overcame his low motivation and wanted to connect with his teammates. He asked Tom how his training was going, and the latter reported that his endurance was where he needed it, and that he was planning to run back to Lenox Square after they were finished. Sam noticed that from the side, Tom even looked thinner than the week before, and asked if he had lost more weight. "Fourteen pounds of fat!" he said proudly, and I've barely started into the Powerbar diet yet. He admitted that he had been doing more running on his running days, and that the hill work was going very well.

As they turned left onto 14th street, and began the last downhill mile to the finish, Suzi became exuberant again. She asked if they could run three minutes and walk one, and the others agreed. She started to pick up the speed as they entered Piedmont Park, but Tom came down on her.

"No Suzi, we're just going to finish and there's still three-quarters of a mile left. You don't know how many people smell the finish line when they enter the park, pick up the pace, and then struggle in."

They glided on the flat above the playing fields and then downhill past the tennis courts together. It was a beautiful day in the park as families and couples strolled and relaxed. Just before the 6 mile mark, the road became flat and the trio ran alongside one another, dodging an occasional roller-blader. They were hot, and tired but glowing with the accomplishment of a challenge that had been met.

Suzi noticed a thin, young man who could have been Tom, about 20 years ago, looking towards them from the shadow of a nearby tree. She instinctively knew that this was Chris. "Tom, do you know him?"

As Tom walked toward the tree, the boy started to walk away. Tom stopped and said "How about a run to Lenox Square." The son stopped, thought for a few long seconds and started running in that direction, with his father.

And the two were off without saying a word. Tom had more bounce in his step than Sam and Suzi had noticed before, and the sillhouets of two athletes disappeared over the hill.

Suzi was enjoying a leisurly morning, reading the Sunday paper, sipping tea, and basking in the glow of the Atlanta's May sunshine—not too cold and not too hot. When she realized that the reduction in her reading light was the shadow of someone standing over her, she took a nervous jump in her seat and gave Tom a bad time for not giving her a more gentle warning.

"I'm finally ready for action after 4 years. Now where is it?"

While she was still thinking about how the article on "Condo Gardens" could apply to her situation, Suzi looked at him with a blank stare. Finally, her left brain got things focused and she said "I've got it!"

"Well, give me the schedule!"

As she looked through her backpack, Suzi continued to make conversation: "Tom, you looked different. This is only the second time I've seen you with a tank top on. You've lost weight, a good bit of weight."

"I've continued to burn it off, Suzi," Tom said with satisfaction. "Eighteen pounds of it." This program of eating powerbars and training so much more easily than I used to do has allowed me to get in my fat-burning distance without injury. Now where's the schedule!"

Suzi enjoyed noticing how Tom tried to look cool and measured while he eagerly tore open the copy of her Galloway Guerrilla Guide to the part on speedwork. As Suzi continued to enjoy her tea and garden article, Tom seemed to catch some of the electricity of the day as a steady stream of folks came into Phidippides to move the fitness part of their busy lives in a positive direction. Tom was in a good mood, and didn't mind sharing his energy with Suzi.

"Just seeing and hearing the runners come and go from the store gets me in the mood for a workout," he said. "When I was competitive, I would come here after work and sit on the curb. There were no nice benches like this. As I saw people come out with more inspiration on their faces than they went in with, it inspired me. Some of the world's great un-recorded workouts of all time took off and finished from this point."

Tom's Fat-burning Program

(Time period: 3 months)

6am: PowerBar, water, and cup of coffee before a 6-8 mile (very slow) jog

8am: 10oz Orange Juice, two bowls of corn flakes, two pieces of toast.(with fake margarine)

9am: 8oz of dilute orange juice on the way to work

10am: Bagel with fat-free cream cheese, 8oz water

11am: PowerBar with 8oz water

12 noon: PowerBar, 8oz water, and 3-4 mile run—accelerations

1:45: 1) bowl of rice and soup in microwave, frenchbread, 8oz dilute fruit juice
2) or rice, salsa, pinto beans, fat-free cottage cheese, with fat-free chips, favorite bottled water—8oz
3) or baked potato, fat-free salad dressing, cottage cheese, whle grain bread

3pm Sourdough bread with fruit (sometimes applesauce), 8oz water

4pm: Snack—(one or two of the following) fat-free saltines, pretzels, baked potato, carrots, celery, banana, apple. 8oz water

5pm: Powerbar, 8oz water, cup of coffe or tea

6pm: hill work or speed work—4-6 miles

7:15: Powerbar, 8oz water (on the way home) from workout

8:00: Pasta with tomato sauce, vegetables and chicken breast, salad (fat-free dressing) french bread 8oz water.

8:45: Fat free cookies, fruit cocktail, or other no-fat dessert

9:30 8oz water

10:45 bedtime

The Galloway Guerrilla Guide:
The Difference Between Speed PLAY vs. Speed WORK

Your vision of how you will conduct your speed training will set your attitude about those sessions, this vision will then determine how involved you are when you do the sessions. For example, the Scandinavians have a significant philosophical difference concerning speed sessions. When Norwegians, Swedes or Finns talk about "speed PLAY," they have a sparkle in their eyes. In contrast, Americans resign themselves to the dreaded versions of speed WORK.

During one of my competitive summers in Europe, I was asked to join fellow runners from several Norwegian running clubs for a session of what they called fartlek (which literally means speed-play). As we gathered, there was a jovial exchange of jokes and stories, and it was obvious that these runners enjoyed the chemistry of running together.

They warned me about the first leader of the pack and when we headed off down the beautiful packed trail system, I was huffing and puffing to hang on to the hardy crew of 15 "greyhound-looking" runners. The locals knew every little dip in the trail, and used it to maximum advantage. The smooth and fast momentum gained from running downhill, pushed them up the next hill. Challenges were made and met at every turn as each picked *his* turn to try to move into the lead.

While we challenged ourselves (often to our limits), I was amazed to find out that we had covered about 10 miles by the end. It seemed more like 7. There were always little circles made to gather the "behinders." We were never running so hard that we couldn't enjoy the scenery the tranquil lakes, or the meadows full of flowers.

If I were to rate the quality and quantity of hard running, it was as good as any speed session I ever ran on the track, in my career, including my training for the Olympics. But five minutes after that speed PLAY had finished, I was already looking forward to joining them for their next one.

Tom glanced over the material which Suzi had provided. After about 5 minutes he had reached an impass.

"Galloway actually recommends several shorter workouts each day which makes sense to these 40+ year-old legs. Can you remember what he said about the multible workouts? This is really different from the gut-busting sessions of my speed work, long and exhausting sessions which left you wiped out, even on the good days! I just assumed that these were necessary for breaking through to the next barrier."

They poured through the Galloway notes and came back to Tom's original observation—that the speed sessions of the future involved several runs on a speed day, instead of one arduous session. Shorter sessions could allow one to *play*. The gut-busting long sessions were *work*.

But several questions raced through Tom's mind which Suzi couldn't answer. Then, Tom noted that an expert in exercise physiology, a professor from Georgia Tech, had just gone into the store. Tom was determined to pin him down as he left the store, so he quickly jotted down his questions. The professor didn't know what hit him when he emerged wearing the latest light-weight top for hot weather.

Dr Druski knew Tom from several years before. They joked about the mistakes they made when both were young and foolish. "I've spent the last 15 years learning the principles of exercise but I still maintain my right to make stupid training mistakes."

Tom showed the "sweat doctor" his main areas of concern from the GGG Speedwork Principle handout.

GGG Speed Training Principles
Setting up a program—to reduce aches and injury—and train muscles to cooperate as a team

1. Break up your speed sessions into 4 components which use slightly different combinations of muscle cells, in different ways: anaerobic runs, accelerations, cruise control runs, and 'shifting gears' sessions (which puts them all together).

2. Shift among the various muscle groups regularly to avoid over-fatigue, injury, and a long recovery time.

3. Start with a small amount of speed play, in each component—below the pace which you could maintain at maximum—to get the muscles used to the activity.

4. Take more rest, (walking) between components, during the beginning phase, than you really need.

5. Back off the workout early before you over-use the muscles. Your goal is to leave the workout feeling like you could do about 25% more. Much of this is accomplished by maintaining a conservative pace in the beginning of the workout.

6. There will be some days when you won't be able to run as fast, and as smooth as on the "good" days. When the muscles aren't responding, don't force yourself to maintain a certain pace. Avoid, at all costs, over-extending the muscles.

"I just don't understand how this works. It's so different from the way I trained."

The professor explained that he didn't agree with everything that Galloway said, but that he noticed two significant principles which popped out of this training plan: 1) multiple workouts which allowed the exercising muscle groups to gradually push beyond their capacity (in a series of small steps) with less chance of overwhelming the main driving muscles, and 2) muscle team-work—specific training for developing the capacity of key muscle groups to get the job done in several different ways.

The concept of multiple workouts had been very successful, offering several advantages over continuous, long interval workouts, while providing a stimulating challenge to the various muscle groups in each activity. If done right, each component wouldn't push the muscles to exhaustion. This reduced the risk of injury and speeded recovery—the main factor which competitive runners neglected—and which slowed down their progress.

"If the muscles have enough time to recover from the last hard day, they will make performance adaptations to handle more effort during the next workout. They'll rebuild stronger. Each workout could enable the runner to increase the efficiency and capacity of the muscles just enough so as not to overwhelm it. This stimulates improvements which increase overall capacity in the next session."

"By targeting specific uses of muscles in each speed session, you're building

teams of muscle cells which can shift activity level and function. By shifting back and forth, you can sustain the performance of the muscles significantly and increase overall performance. In contrast, you'll fatigue the muscles faster if they're used in the same way for an extended period. Anyone in sports knows that teamwork among players can lead to a level of play greater than the sum of the talent of the individuals. These sessions build upon one another, develop muscular teamwork, and produce race performances which are even greater than the individual speed sessions would predict."

"Let me see if I'm getting it," said Tom, "to enhance performance, multiple workouts conditioned the muscle cells to handle an increasing capacity in several different ways. By working as a 'team,' the various groups could coax out more performance than the steady, continuous use of the same primary groups as individuals."

As Dr. Druski interpreted the Galloway program to Tom, he seemed to get more and more "into" the discussion and asked for the GGG handout which Suzi had picked up during the past summer's fitness vacation. As his wife started honking for him to go, Druski explained that he needed to pick up his kids from the weekend soccer wars. His parting thoughts were that the GGG workouts could produce the same conditioning as the more rigorous and more fatiguing sessions usually done on the track.

The thoughts kept coming as he closed the door. "Tom, our 40 year-old-recovery rate is significantly slower than it was

A Galloway Guerrilla Program for Tom

Goal: A faster 5K, and stamina for a 10K
Starting Point: The first week's level of exercise is about what you are doing, as I gather from Suzi.

Mon	Tue	Wed	Thurs	Fri	Sat	Sun
Week I						
V.easy 3-4mi 3-5mi accelerations	Easy 5-6mi 3-4 mi speed play	XT	Easy 5-6mi 3-4mi accelerations	Easy 5-6mi track play	off off	long and easy
Week II						
Easy 3-5mi Easy 3-5mi	XT	Easy 5-6mi 3-4mi accel	Easy 5-6mi track play	off off	5Krace 6-9mi	XT
Week III						
Easy 5-6mi 3-4mi accel	Easy 5-6mi 3-5mi speed play	XT	Easy 7-9mi 3-4mi accel	off	long and easy	XT

* This is a three week rotation. The fourth week would be a repetition of the first.

* Two sessions are scheduled each day. The first one is a warm-up, and the second is the improvement stimulator. If you have to combine them, use the first part of the afternoon workout as an extended warmup, running about 1-2 minutes per mile slower than you usually run on a slow day. During the last part, you may work into the faster running.

* If you have the time and a flexible schedule, you can add a 2-3 mile run at noontime with light accelerations. This really gets the legs ready for the afternoon speedwork.

Notes:
1. "Easy" means at least 2 minutes per mile slower than you could run that distance on that day. "v. easy" means at least 3 minutes per mile slower than you could run.

2. XT means 45-90 minutes of any combination of the following activities (you may spread them out throughout the day—no need to do them all at once): Running in the water, Nordic Track, swimming, weights, rowing machine, cycling, etc., but no stair machines, empact aerobics, etc. If you only have 15-30 minutes to cross-train, DO IT!

3. Off days could include some light XT, just maximize recovery of the legs. Swimming, walking and light upper-body weights would be fine, for example.

4. Speed Play: 3-6 miles on the roads or trails on rolling terrain; be sure to warm-up and warm down with an easy mile of each. Start with approximately one mile, slightly slower than current 5K race pace, with 3-4 easy accelerations of 100-300 meters each, coming back to the pace you started the mile. On the additional mile (or so) segments, pick up the speed to current 5K race pace, and just extend the length of the accelerations as you feel comfortable. Shoot for 3-5 accelerations per mile.

5. Accelerations (accel): work on quicker turnover. Keep feet lower to the ground and encourage a quick response from the ankle, which will make running easier and faster. Think of taking a very light touch with the foot. Don't lift the knees, don't push up into the air. Stay close to the ground with quick rhythm. Don't overstride and risk an overstretch of the hamstring; and please don't push so far on each acceleration that you fatigue the muscles. Ease off before you reach fatigue. See the section on "form accelerations," in the chapter, "Putting it Together."

6. Long and Easy—just that! Since your longest in the last two weeks has been 12 miles, you could start with 13-14 miles and increase by 2 miles every other week until you reach 15-16 miles. That's as long as you need to go for the 10K. You must run these long ones at least 2 minutes per mile slower than you could run that distance on that day. Any faster than that will compromise your recovery and keep you from feeling as good as you could during your track play and speed play sessions to come. Running the long one too fast will also keep you from recovering as quickly.

7. Track Play—(similar to speed play, but on a 400 meter track). After a warmup of 1-2 miles, go to a track and do 4-6 laps of accelerating the straightaways and jogging the curves. When your legs feel ready for action, run segments of 1-1.5 miles at desired race pace. During each of these, accelerate smoothly for 200-400 meters and glide afterward. Walk and jog between segments. Build up to 10-12 laps of segments.

8. You may need more warmup on some speed days. Instead of one easy mile, take 2 or three miles and extend the total workout by that amount. When you run these extra miles, however, do them very slowly. As we get older, we can often do the same quality we did 10 years before if we get adequate blood flow into the muscles early, and gradually ease into the workout without any straining. Another factor which will help those "over 35 year-olds" recover faster is to put more rest into the workout between the hard parts by walking more between the segments.

10 years ago and the muscles can't handle heavy workloads. This just might be the way for runners over 40 to stay competitive with the younger crowd." Before he could start another sentence, Mrs. Druski was driving out of the Ansley Mall parking lot.

As he left, Tom walked Suzi to her car saying that he liked the concept of several short sessions. "It's like recess— in school. I lived for recess."

"You men, noted Suzi, "you were always looking for a chance to play!"

"No. I'm used to speedwork being hard work and I'm having trouble buying this because it just seems too easy."

"I knew that this was going to happen, said Suzi, "so I sent Jeff Galloway a note about you. That's why I asked you all those questions about your training last week. He faxed this back to me yesterday with a caution that you back off at the first sign of overwork or possible injury."

Tom was interested and thankful that Suzi had gone to the trouble to help him—and he absorbed the sheet like a dry sponge in water.

Suzi enjoyed seeing Tom's excitement and his emotional response to many of the speed sessions and tips on the training sheet. In her work, she had learned to appreciate the moment when an individual was able to really feel the communication coming from the speaking, writing, video, etc. Tom was totally immersed in the training program.

"If this works. I can get back in shape without nearly the aches and pains and injuries which I thought were just part of the process. On the other hand, I don't think I believe this. It's just too easy."

When Suzi asked him what he had done wrong in the past, Tom explained.

"My mistaken view was that a speed session had to be a WORK-out, that it had to shock my system into improvements; the greater the shock, the greater the improvement. When I had a great session, it was often too much for my level of conditioning and was followed by continued fatigue, burnout or injury. Yet, I congratulated myself for over-doing it. This Galloway Program is certainly challenging but is a kinder and gentler path of progress. We who are 'challenged by age', must avoid the interruptions which I thought were just

part of the process. By gently increasing the capacity of the muscles, lungs, blood system, energy supply, fat burning, anaerobic waste removal, the systems learn to work together."

"It also seems to me," said Suzi, "that the rest between the fast sections gives the muscles a chance to rebuild and get ready for the next challenge."

"On those few days that I've run hard this Spring, I've been a bit discouraged about how long it has taken to recover. Days off from running are much more important at age 42 than they were at 32. But I'm beginning to see how it is possible to combine enough significant speed with significant rest, and maybe— just maybe—run as fast as I did 10 years ago."

"Why don't you reserve judgement on the ease of this," said Suzi, "until you've tried it."

Tom was starting his slow warm-up when he heard Suzi's voice behind him. He ran over to her car and noticed that the third amigo wasn't there

"Sam assured me that he would do his 3-4 mile "cruise" today, explained Suzi, "but he just couldn't break away this morning."

"I'm getting this funny feeling that Sam isn't working out, that he's avoiding us because of stress or something," offered Tom.

"I can't deny that I've had those thoughts," noted Suzi, "but I keep thinking that my professional conscience is making me too sensitive. I've done this before. Where's Chris?"

"He's around. He still hasn't opened up to me. It's funny, he'll go through the workout, seeming to be in good spirits. Before and afterward, however, he complains about everything. I tell him that he doesn't have to do it but he keeps coming back. "We've gotten in some good training, and some good converstation, but not much communication."

As Suzi got out of her car, Tom commented that she was thinner. Suzi beamed and then retorted, "I suppose that means that you thought I was really fat before." Tom chose not to respond to that one.

Suzi asked for more information about the communication problem with Chris, who was warming up on the other side of the field. Tom explained that this would be a critical workout for their relationship. Chris would be shy for most of their time together, saying almost nothing. Then, when they sat down at Morrison's for a light snack afterward, Chris would start his critical analysis of everything, picking it apart.

Suzi used this opportunity to give Tom a bad time. "Morrisons, with all the healthy vegetables and things. That's no fun. No wonder he was negative."

"My ex-wife has that negative streak in her also. I guess that this is the way both of them choose to relate to other people."

"It's pretty normal for an adolescent to do that," noted Suzi, "especially if he has a role model."

"Have you tried calling his hand on this criticial behavior pattern?"

"I'm afraid he'll go away."

"There's always that chance, but your relationship will move forward in an honest direction. And you could also take the lead as he starts to criticize. Reinforce him for his progress, for anything he's done well. By taking a positive lead, you can set the tone for the communication."

As Chris ran up, Tom introduced him to Suzi, and the trio took off to complete their workout. Suzi was very quickly on her own.

The Warm-Up

Walk 5-10 minutes
Cruise for 5-10 minutes (jog very slowly for 2 minutes, and walk for 30-60 seconds)
Jog for 10 minutes
2-4 laps of accelerations (jog the curves, and accelerate on the straights)
Walk for 3 minutes
Start the workout

Tom told Chris that he was free to run faster if he felt that his old Dad was holding him back. The father cautioned, however, that he'd do better at the end of the speed-play, if he paced himself early.

Suzi's Speed Play

4 x 400 meter (once around the track) accelerating for 200 meters and coasting for 200 meters
(walk for one 400 meter lap between)
4 x 100 meter hill, with a very gentle grade, near the track

Play with a quick turnover, keeping stride length from getting too long. Do not sprint!
(Walk down the hill, and walk until recovered at the bottom—before starting the next one)

Suzi had built up to this workout over the past 4 weeks, starting with 1 each of the 400's and the hills. As she got into her workout, so did "the boys."

Tom sensed that Chris seemed to have a chip on his shoulder, although the young fellow didn't say a word as they slowly jogged 400 meters. Over the next mile, Tom would accelerate for 100 meters and then jog for 100 meters. This made Chris more impatient. Tom tried to explain that this not only warmed up the muscles, but that it started the process of shifting between the various functions required of the muscle groups. By activating and conditioning them now, they could call them into action during races. At first, Chris would get far ahead on the acceleration and have to walk or jog extra slowly to allow Tom to catch up. By the end, Tom was running smooth on the accelerations, with Chris a bit ahead but running with a "jerky" motion.

Once he was warmed up, Tom had mastered the technique of shifting off of the accelerating muscles to cruise control or gliding muscles. He was running almost as fast as on the accelerations, but with less effort. As he noticed Chris huffing and puffing, Tom tried to explain the gliding technique, but to no avail. By the end of the acceleration session, Chris was breathing heavily to stay just ahead of Tom who had learned to recover on each of the glide segments with a smooth and quick turnover.

"The boys" were set up to run three segments of a rolling road loop which was .75 mile long. They would start at their current 5K race pace. Tom assumed the lead and would accelerate for 200 meters and then glide for 300 meters. As the speed session progressed, Tom felt his muscles loosen up, and his legs respond to each challenge whether it be an uplift in terrain or an acceleration from Chris. Tom's form was so smooth on the last one that Chris couldn't tell when the older runner was accelerating. The subtle surprise of Tom moving alongside aggravated Chris who had a problem giving up the lead. On the last segment, Chris tried to stay ahead at any cost, and tired himself out much more quickly by over-responding to each of Tom's challenges. At the end, Tom lightly accelerated up a series of three hills. Chris kept up on the first two and couldn't handle the third, slowing down dramatically in self-perceived defeat.

Suzi was finishing up her session as Chris and Tom entered the athletic field and stopped on the other side of the track. She sensed an argument, and watched Chris storm off. Suzi jogged around to Tom and asked what happened.

"Chris is having trouble with the unpredictability of these speed-play workouts. He was programmed from the years of his youth track team, to run hard on the track, knowing exactly when to work hard and when to let up. He got used to this. In races, he has always had problems because one never knows when the opponent is going to let up, or push ahead. Our workout today helps prepare runners for the physical and mental demands of the shift in effort needed in racing. Chris just didn't want to cope with this."

"What did he do?" asked Suzi.

"He exploded; told me that this workout wasn't helping him and that no good athlete in this country does this kind of work. He stormed off when I responded that there was only one American in my generation who ran this way, Steve Prefontaine."

"Does Chris know the story of Prefontaine?"

"He received an award for a biography research essay on 'Pre' when he was a senior in high school. It was the only writing project Chris ever well. 'Pre' was Chris' hero."

"Pre"
The Legend Lives On

Steve Prefontaine came from a tough small town on the Oregon coast. He worked hard at track and cross country from the very first day—and became the best high school distance runner in Oregon. This wasn't enough. 'Pre' wanted to be "the best", period.

During his senior year at Marshville High School in Coos Bay, 'Pre' set national High School records including an 8:41 two mile.

Under the guidance of the University of Oregon's world-class distance running coach, Bill Bowerman, 'Pre' worked his way to the top of the US lists.

Pre was a charismatic athlete which the press followed throughout track seasons in the early 70's. He would challenge his competitors, daring them to run his race.

He became the hero of thousands of boys who formed the nucleus of the first running boom in the late 1970's.

Sam walked up to the door of the President's office at Georgia International University. The receptionist was at lunch, but the door was cracked open and President Dowel, who was moving around inside, spotted Sam outside. Sam heard him call his "boss," Bill Palmer.

"Come on in, Sam, we need to do some brainstorming for next year now that the students have gone home. I've asked Dr. Palmer to join us and he promised to hurry up here."

After a very awkward 5 minutes, Palmer walked through the door wearing athletic gear, with a towel draped over his shoulder.

"Pardon my towel, Sam, just got back from my racquetball game. It's getting harder and harder to beat the young guys. Say, are you doing any exercise yet. after your heart attack."

"I'm trying to do the Peachtree Road Race, "answered Sam."

"Now Sam, that's real strenuous. I know because I do it every year, but I'm in shape. You've never been much for physical stuff—I'd watch that. Otherwise, tell me how you're doing."

"I'm adjusting, Dr. Palmer, but I really miss my project on primitive man."

President Dowel walked back in the room, sat down, and took command of the discussion.

"One of the—THE toughest part of my job, Sam, is allocating resources—funds, buildings, people—but the greatest challenge is people. I strive for a win-win situation, but with our financial situation being what it is, a growing percentage of the time, I must deal with someone losing out. It's my job to choose what is best for the university."

Knowing that nothing he could say would make any difference, Sam acknowledged that the university was in a difficult situation. The president then let Palmer do all of the talking.

"Sam, this heart problem of yours couldn't have come at a worse time, a time when we need all of our professors to be working at 150% capacity. I'm going to have to readjust the assignments in several departments especially since we are eliminating your Archeology Studies program. We're also going to have to cut back, and eliminate positions. There will be a number of good professors, like you, who will have to leave the university, because we just can't pay them. Now because everybody likes you—especially your students— I'm going to offer you a special status, a full-time half professorship. Now this seems like it's a contradiction—but it means that your area of expertise can only fill up three classes—which is now half of the new workload for full professors. You will of course continue to receive all medical benefits, etc."

"Does this mean that my pay will be cut in half?"

"Yes."

"How do you expect me to make my mortgage payments on that."

"Sam, many of your friends will not have this option."

Sam was stunned. The flux of conflicting emotions left him powerless to respond to Palmer's statement. Out of his gut rolled the only response he could muster, one that had been simmering for months. This time he addressed the president, looking him straight in the eye.

"Wasn't it your firm which invested the university's assets in derivitives, and got us into this financial jam in the first place."

The immaculately dressed busiessman-president cleared his throat and proceeded with a statement he had been reciting for months.

"Sam, I wasn't part of the group which managed those assets. I was brought in as a donation to the university. My salary is paid by the firm. I've worked with numerous 'turn-around' situations before. We'll make it here, we just need to tighten our belts. We look upon you as an invaluable asset, and don't want to lose you."

Back in his office, Sam just stared at his desk, piled high with papers and tests which needed final grades. But Sam just stared, with no expression on his face, no energy. He let the phone ring twice before he slowly walked to the wall phone next to the office bulletin board covered in memos, post-its, and family pictures.

"Oh, Don, thanks for calling. How is the soccer season going for your kids. Yea, you and Marilyn need to take another trip with us to Buffalo so that we can have a summer snow vacation again. Oh yea, I sent you the life insurance contract because you've been such a good friend in helping us look over the contract on our house for re-financing. Well, I've got another question for you. Since I had my heart attack, I've started thinking about these things and I wondered what the exceptions are for paying my family if something ever happened to me.

OK. OK. the normal ones, such as suicide.

After he hung up, Sam noted that his secretary had clipped an article from the

Atlanta News and hi-lited a section for him. Something really grabbed his interest and he read it very carefully.

If You're Running Peachtree—DON'T.

Even if you have a very healthy heart you'll put yourself at risk by overzealous behavior when it's hot and humid. By avoiding the following, you can reduce the chance of heat disease, injury, and even death. Don't spend Peachtree day in the hospital.

Don't work out during the heat of the day. High heat and high humidity are a deadly mix.

If you've chosen the coolest time of the day and it's still hot,
- Don't run hard
- Don't run in the direct sun
- Don't run hills

Don't wear heavy clothing, such as sweat clothes, long pants or tops with long sleeves.

Don't consume caffeine or alcohol before exercising

Don't go an hour without drinking 8oz. of water, sports drink or juice (every hour you are awake.)

Suzi tried to explain to Tom that she didn't feel like running, that it had been a terrible day at work. After a string of stressful situations with clients, she received official notification that government funding had been cut off for a program which paid for over 30% of her clients. She couldn't drop many of these people, and yet she absolutely had to have the income.

"Look, there are more important things in this world than my exercise. Take Sam. He hasn't run in almost 2 weeks because of stress at the university. They're trying to push him out, to hire young professors who cost less. He's really down and I can't get him to go out there with me."

Tom told Suzi that he had just ended a long stretch of stress at work. He quit. At first Suzi was surprised, then angry.

"I can't believe this. What is it with you 40 plus runners? You think that you can just live off the land or something."

"I've just had enough," Tom said with a mixed tone of relief and anger. "I'm asked to back up a philosophy which the company uses to sell its services, and then my boss undermines me by cutting costs, providing inferior products, changing things around, and then ordering me to make amends with the client. Almost every day is spent in negociation and I'm burned out. Yes, I yearn to pursue the simple goal of beating Dylan at Peachtree."

Sam gets out of his car and looks up at the long final hill leading up to Piedmont Hospital with nervousness and dread. His sweatshirt is already wet around the neck and in the center of the chest and back as he begins to lumber along. With the eyes of a man on a mission, he pushes his legs hard, lifting the knees. By the time he reaches the top, his legs are tight, the arms are pumping, and his breathing is almost out of control.

Annoyed that he was able to do the first

Getting Used To Heat and Humidity

Stay away from heat most of the time. Most of your exercise sessions should be done in the coolest time possible, usually just before and just after dawn.

Make sure you've received a doctor's clearance for exercising in hot weather. Almost no one is excluded, but you want to make sure. Pick a doctor who thoroughly knows the effects and benefits of exercise.

Be sure to drink water often during hot and humid weather. Keep a container of water with you all day long and drink small amounts, regularly, about 6-8 oz. per hour, indoors. If you're sweating, then increase the amount of water.

To get an exercising body used to the heat and humidity, exercise during the warm part of the day, once a week. At first, go only for about 4-5 minutes. Gradually increase the amount of warm exercise by 3-4 minutes each week, until you can do 20-25 minutes in the heat and humidity.

Beware of Heat Disease. At the first sign of heat problems ease your effort and cool off. Heat disease symptoms include—but are not limited to the following—hot and cold flashes, cessation of sweating, clammy skin, loss of control over muscles, and extreme heat build-up, particularly in the area of the head, and nausea.

one without more anguish, Sam jogs and walks down to his starting area, in a sweatshirt and sweatpants which are totally soaked in perspiration. As he starts up the second hill, the heavy breathing starts immediately. Less than half way up, much to his disappointment, Sam's leg muscles are so tight that he slows down. By the time he reaches the top, he's still breathing hard, but has had to slow down due to total leg fatigue.

On the third one, Sam struggles hard during the first part of the hill and has to walk, because his legs are so tight and tired. He tries two more times, and can't go far enough to give him the exertion level he was tryng for.

Sam continued to sweat as he leaned against his car, feeling like a failure in many ways. But as the over-exertion wore off and the body temperature went down, he felt better. By the time he was in his driveway, his mind had shifted into the pleasant endorphin relaxation which produced a sense of satisfaction. Sam was surprised. He hadn't felt a similar sense of satisfaction about anything he had done since the run on the course with Suzi and Tom. But as he walked into the house, he shifted back to the hard reality of trying to explain a very difficult situation to his wife and family.

Seated at his kitchen table sifting through papers and empty PowerBar wrappers, Tom saw Chris at the front door and motioned him in, saying that he had to make one more call. Chris asked what he was doing, and Tom replied that he had quit his job and was organizing his possibilities into three categories: 1)former clients at his old company, 2)contacts he had met who didn't do business with his former company, and 3) clients of his former company who might have business in areas not covered by his former company. At that moment, the phone rang.

Tom explained to the caller that he was no longer with the Fitness Company, that he was setting up consulting services in areas not covered by his former company, he had no desire to compete with them.

When he finished with the call, Chris asked Tom, with a puzzled look on his face: "Aren't you scared. You know, starting all over."

"Scared isn't quite the word," noted Tom. Hey, let's go out and run. Tom took one more sip of his coffee, put on his speed shoes and they were out the door.

Chris started his jog too fast for Tom. The father gently instructed the son in the subtle and not subtle pacing adjustments which runners make as they age.

"What you mean to say," said Chris in a kidding tone, "is that old men require more time for the legs to warm up."

Track Play

In that 1.5 mile jog to the track, Tom told about his prospects, and Chris described his study plan at Georgia State. As they got into the accelerations at the track,

Tom and Chris's Warm-Up

1. Jog slowly for 1.5 miles: starting at 2-3 minutes per mile slower than 5K race pace

2. Walk for 2-5 minutes, doing light massage on key muscles and sometimes a few light stretches

3. 4-6 laps of accelerations: picking up pace on the straights, and jogging or cruising the curves. The accelerations started out at 10K race pace and the last ones were a little faster than 5K race pace.

4. Walk for 2-3 minutes and start the workout

Chris asked polite questions which Tom instantly read as insecurity about the main workout.

As they started the accelerations, Chris and Tom began to open up with one another. Chris admitted that he really didn't want to go to college, but he knew his mother would make it miserable for him, otherwise. He finally realized that this was his opportunity to get away from her for a while. Tom was proud of himself for not making any editorial comments.

As he started to sweat, during the second acceleration, Tom admitted that he WAS scared about his work prospects. While he had lots of contacts, there was no one who seemed to have any real work in his major interest area: setting up behavioral health promotion programs which tied into insurance, productivity, and team-building. Undoubtedly, as a small business owner, he would have to mold his services to the needs of his customer.

"All of the companies are talking about health promotion, but nobody I've talked to has any power to put a program into place. Yes, Chris, I feel great insecurity, but 6 months ago I wouldn't have even taken the plunge. I like the thought that I'm trying. The catalyst has been my running. As soon as I got the first 10 pounds off and the competitive juices flowing, a switch was turned on. I've got focus, drive and the energy to see it through. And yes, I'm scared."

Tom noticed that Chris was trying to run too fast on the next-to-last acceleration and got him to cut his stride length about an inch. Chris was surprised, admitting

that this stopped the jerkiness in his form and allowed him to run faster.

On the 5 minute walk, Tom talked Chris through the speed session.

"We're probably going to do, 4 repetitions. But focus on one at a time, forgetting the others. Each will be two and a half to three laps in length. We'll go out at 5K race pace on the first lap, increase pace on the second one, through turnover and NOT stride length, then hang on and glide through the next lap or half lap, trying to maintain a pace that is close to the pace of the accleration, but without pushing.

Chris had trouble with the glide and Tom explained that the concept was to maintain turnover from the faster lap, while letting the legs relax. Tom explained that he was just learning how to do it too, but when he did it right, he moved with strength and good turnover, but without straining.

"Sorta like coasting down a hill?" asked Chris.

"Yes, there was some effort required, but only a fraction of that needed for the hard acceleration."

On the first one, Chris held himself back but Tom sensed that he was frustrated and wanted to lead. Since both were training to run a 5K in 5 minute-per-mile pace, they were right on schedule with a first lap in 75 seconds. As Tom started to accelerate, Chris lengthened out his stride and easily took the lead, running the second lap in 68 with Tom two seconds back. They glided through the third lap in 73.

It was time for Chris to take the lead. Tom cautioned him again about the need to pace oneself, by going out at a reasonable pace. Tom was not surprised, however, to watch Chris glide through a tour of the track in 68 seconds, then accelerate to a 64, and glide to a 72. Tom was proud to see Chris look like a champion, smooth, strong and confident. But he chided the younger athlete for not running the assigned pace.

"Look, I've got it today. By running faster in this workout, I'll develop the capacity to run even faster in the races. You may not believe this, but I do."

Tom explained that in a few weeks, he might be ready for that speed session, but that this pace would probably cause him to tie-up and lose the good consistent effect of the last part of the speed play. But the crash came sooner.

On the third rep, Chris took over the lead half-way through the first lap. He ran a 68, then a 65 and then the muscles rebelled. He struggled in with a 77 on the last one, complaining about his tight muscles.

Chris tried to run the fourth rep, but had to drop out after the first lap. Tom run a smooth 75, 71, 73. As he joined Chris on the warm down, Tom could sense some tension. By the time they had covered 2 miles, Chris opened up saying that this wasn't his type of workout—that he didn't feel comfortable doing these variable pace things. When Tom tried to explain the concept again, Chris became very defensive.

"I think these workouts are designed for old runners like you. I'm young and strong and can run more explosive workouts. I'm sorry. My muscles feel like they're holding back on this workout, and they can't do what they're capable of doing."

"Look, Suzi. I don't know how serious his condition is. Dr Life just called saying that Sam had collapsed on Peachtree while running. I didn't bother to ask further, I thought we should get down there.

The 10 minute drive from Suzi's place dragged on with each stoplight holding them three times as long as usual, or so it seemed. Suzi tried to pass the time by talking about Chris, but Tom didn't open up about their most recent dispute after the speed play. Just before they got to Peachtree Hospital, Tom shed the latest light on the sore subject.

"Chris wants to get back into running, like I do. I can feel his desire to express himself through these speed sessions. I just don't know whether he can't deal with me and the 'father' relationship, or whether he just can't handle my concept of speed play. My intuition tells me that that he's using the workouts to get out of an awkward situation in dealing with me. I just heard through the grapevine that he's joined a workout group headed by Brian Masimi, Dylan's coach.

After parking the car, Suzi and Tom raced one another upstairs to the heart center and waited anxiously until "Dr. Life" came race-walking down the corridor.

"The bad news, said Lifowitz, "is that Sam suffered a form of heat exhaustion. I've got him under observation now. Come in to my office for a chat."

Tom noticed that the office had evolved since his last visit, some pictures down, some new ones up, and lots of new quotes and sayings.

"You haven't called for a run, Tom," the doctor began, "although I see that you've been running."

"How do you know?" asked Suzi.

"Sunken cheeks, 20 maybe 23 pounds lighter, sunken eyes that have some fire in them which wasn't there three months ago."

"Look, this may seem like a strange story," Life began, "and I can't get any information out of his wife, but I think that Sam tried to commit suicide by running."

"He has been going out during the

hottest time of the day and running as hard as he can up the worst hill on the Peachtree course. He took off his heart monitor during these sessions, and when the nurse called him on the time lapses, he lied, saying he was taking a shower, or something."

The instant reality hit Suzi hard. Her professional "shrink" warning signals had been going off independently during the last two weeks as she processed each bit of information, and she hadn't put them together. She explained her analysis to the others based upon the following signals.

1. Increasingly depressed mood
2. Major job stress, with no good options
3. Financial stress resulting from income loss
4. Not joining workouts with her and Tom
5. Giving her a hint by saying he was doing some 'hard hill work'

"It's really an ironic situation," commented the doctor, "because the angioplasty and exercise has really worked. He's not even close to a heart problem now. You, the training team, have really whipped him into shape. It was the heat that got him. He even weighs 18 lbs. less than he did 3 months ago.

"Is it possible to catch a temporary heart problem," asked Suzi, "to lose that kind of fat?"

The three of them conspired and planned a strategy to help Sam get through his job crisis. Dr. Life said that his goal of Peachtree is more important than ever. Tom said that he could identify with him on the job front. Suzi said that she knew a lawyer who might be able to help Sam, a public defender who owes Suzi many favors, because she has helped many of his "clients," including testifying in court for them.

When Tom heard who it was, he laughed. "Crazy Jim. No way." Tom told of several of Jim's creative courtroom situations which had not worked, but had entertained the judge and jury.

They went in to see Sam, who looked tired, and a bit sheepish. He had an IV and heart monitor, but otherwise, looked normal.

"So you were trying to sneak in some extra training on us," said Tom.

"I guess I over-did it," answered Sam.

They talked about what was new, and Tom mentioned his resignation followed immediately by a statement that he was already on the track of a better job. When Sam said he missed their workouts together, Suzi asked him if he'd like to go to the Home Depot 5K with them. Sam looked at Dr. Life, who agreed, provided he not wear sweat clothes. Sam looked very sheepish again.

As they walked out of the hospital together, Dr Lifowitz continued to ask Tom about his running program, speedwork, goals for Peachtree and more. When Tom mentioned that he still needed to get in his run—even if it was 10pm, the doctor offered to take him on a tour of the residential neighborhoods around the hospital. Tom realized that he was already dressed: he had been wearing running shorts as underwear for several weeks now, and he had his running shoes on. So after a visit to the physicians locker room, they were off.

started each run at 8:30 per mile—but on many of my runs the legs wouldn't feel so great after 1-3 miles. So I slowed down to 10 minutes per mile for the first mile—and what a difference. On most days, I speed up at the end—but on virtually every session—I feel great. Starting slowly makes all the difference in how I feel on that run".

When the good doctor mentioned that he was having the most enjoyable running year of his life, Tom begged for his secrets: "While I am getting better at running slower from the beginning of my runs—and taking more days off from running, there are still many days when my legs just don't feel good at any time during the run—and I only feel better during the 'afterglow' when the warmdown has been completed."

"You may not be starting out slowly enough." noted Lifowitz, "Five years ago, I thought I was running slow when I

Tom had, in his own mind, placed Dr. Life into the category of a slow jogger. And while the beginning pace was 9+ minutes per mile, they had gradually increased to about 7 minute pace. Dr. Life was running smoothly at this speed—which caused Tom to breath more heavily than the Doctor.

"By running significantly slower in the beginning, my 'over 40' legs can warm up, and the whole body can be gently introduced to exercise. I have no proof of this, but it seems that the endorphins start flowing very quickly when I run slowly, producing a wonderful feeling of well-being. I know for a fact that my right brain—you know, the wacky part of us—gets activated more quickly. It starts dumping interesting, humorous, and entertaining thoughts—sometimes so quickly that I can't keep up trying to enjoy them. They race through my conciousness quickly, as if your dreams could zoom across a thought screen. Sometimes I just chuckle and laught during the whole run. This doesn't happen, however, when I run faster."

"But why do the runs on some mornings seem so much harder?" asked Tom, "I had one of those this morning."

"There are several reasons why you feel better or worse—especially after sleeping: dehydration, diet, and mental rehearsal. As we age, our metabolism rate slows down, and all three of these make you feel worse that you would feel under the same circumstances when you were younger. By 'mental rehearsal', I mean that most of us negatively prepare ourselves for the next day— telling ourselves in advance that we will feel bad in the morning. Just as this negative programming helps to bring it about, you can positively rehearse feeling up-beat, and getting the metabolism rate kicked up so that you will! We can also helpourselves along with a few more somewhat natural hormone injections"

"Salt is another culprit. Even one salty meal the night before can leave you quite dehydrated the next morning. Try to limit your night time eating to foods which you know do not have added salt. Pasta is usually fine—but the sauce is often loaded with salt."

"Since I've started running very early in the morning, I instinctively began turning to PowerBars and fresh fruit as my night time diet of choice. Very rarely

Avoiding the Slow Morning Syndrome

Dehydration
Caffeine, alcohol, and salty food will dehydrate you—even if you are drinking lots of water throuughout the day. Avoiding these three within 4 hours of bedtime will help—followed by regular doses of water—4-6 oz per hour.

Alcohol is a central nervous system depressant and will give the 'blaghs' anyway. The more you consume, the more difficult it will be to get your body (and spirit) feeling good the next morning.

Upon waking, drink 4-6 oz of water every 30 minutes and avoid consuming any caffeine for at least an hour and a half.

If I've had a glass of wine the night before, I will eat a powerbar soon after rising (with water) and have a cup of coffee about 90 minutes after getting out of bed. That 'revs' me up.

Diet
Most folks don't realize the difference one night-time meal can make on their attitude, and feeling of well-being the next day. The negative effect increases as we get older, only partially due to the slowing down of the metabolism rate.

Young people will even feel sluggish the morning after a very fatty evening meal and this effect increases with age. Fat slows down blood flow, and many other systems in the body—and it will definitely make you feel bad on morning runs—or on afternoon runs after a heavy business lunch.

do I have negative mornings due to diet any more.

Mental Rehearsal

If you limit the negative effects of dehydration and diet, you can exert about a 60-95% influence over how you feel the next morning—through mental rehearsal. Most of us do this negatiively right now. By telling ourselves that we'll feel bad the next morning—we set the stage for it to happen.

If you mentally rehearse feeling good—you will. As you learn how to be a more effective rehearser, you will mold your attitude, indeed, your entire morning environment.

For three hours before you go to bed, spend a few minutes each hour mentally rehearsing your morning attitude as you get moving. You'll awakeN at the time you need; feeling sleepy, but you take action by sitting up. Yes, you feel groggy, but you get up and walk to the bathroom to drink some water. Then you put on shorts and running clothes and shoes—as you go about your 'wake-up' ritual. Through each part of your rehearsal, go through positive thoughts
'I'm feeling better'
'I'm feeling good now'
'I feel alive'
.....and so forth.

By constructing a mental environment which is realistic but positive—you mold the way you will feel the next morning. You're setting up a series of small steps which lead to one another. Mental rehearsal sets up the positive processes which start happening almost automatically each morning as you go through the process over and over. This is very powerful stuff.

"But what about the other factors which affect runners as they age—like recovery rate...is there anything you can do about it."

About the only thing I do medically is take some ibupropin when I've had a hard session. By taking it immediately after the hard or long session, I've recovered almost as fast as when I was in my 20's.

When Tom asked if the doctor recommended that he use ibupropin under the same circumstances, "Life" said that Tom should talk to his doctor first.

The other factors that Lifowitz had found to help him recover fast, feel good and run well were on a list which the doctor gave Tom afterward.

Feeling Better as you Get Older

1. Significant days off from running:
   for those 25-35: 2 days off from running
   for those 35-45: 3 days off from running
   for those above 45: every other day running program

2. Extra slow starts to each run:
   walk for 5 minutes, first
   jog for 5 minutes (about 3+ minutes per mile slower than you could run the run's length)
   ease into the workout pace and never force the muscles to perform when tired, tight, etc

3. Extra slow long runs
   at least 2 minutes per mile slower than you could run that distance on that day (be sure to adjust for heat, humidity, hills, etc)
   walking breaks—one minute walks every 3-5 minutes, from the beginning
   the slower you go, the faster you recover—yet you receive the same endurance

4. Form adjustments
   keep from over-striding—especially downhill, in speed sessions, at end of races (shuffle along close to the ground)
   don't bounce, keep feet low to the ground
   don't get up on your toes—work on quick turnover of feet and legs instead

5. Treat any possible injury—as an injury
   Take an extra day (or more) off from running
   Use ice regularly—a chunk of ice, rubbed directly on the skin
   Ask your doctor about an anti-inflammatory, such as ibupropin

6. Don't let the left brain push you into over-training
   As we get older, we are able to mentally focus and concentrate
   The logical left brain can push us harder and further than we are ready on a given day try to stay under the intuitive control of the right brain

The doctor had been waiting for over twenty years for this moment, but he was in better shape than Tom, and he knew it. As Lifowitz got into his instruction, the pace picked up. When they had covered about 3.5 miles, Tom wasn't able to catch his breath to ask a question. Realizing that this was happening to one of his former heros, Lifowitz slowed down and told stories about running in the 70's, and how medicine has changed. By the time they were climbing back toward Peachtree Hospital, Tom had 'burned off' all his stress—and was very impressed with the transformation which had occurred in his companion—from a high school running geek, to a world class medical expert, and a great human being.

"Sam meet Jim Dobbins." Suzi gestured

"You mean 'Crazy Jim' said Tom.

As Sam was saying ""Look, I don't want to stir up anything..."The others were renewing their acquaintance—and remembering some fun times from two different parts of Jim's life. Jim talked infor-

mally with Sam about his problem with the university—and Sam simply stated the facts. Jim followed up with a few questions about how he had been handled some information about the grant he had received from the National Science foundation, etc. While he said that there might be a legal case for Sam, Jim said that he would have to research it first.

As Suzi and Tom were standing, waiting for Sam, a man about 50 recognized Tom and started talking.

"Hey, Tom, you're the one who got me into this—if it weren't for you, I'd be pleasantly sleeping right now."

When Tom didn't seem to recognize him, the man went on to say that his insurance company had sent him to a retreat

for corporate "key people" 7 years ago. Tom had set up a lifestyle program of low-fat eating, exercise, and motivational sessions which got him and several of the others on the road. He also mentioned that he has used many of the ideas Tom presented in his present position—

"I'm in charge of the 'fast break' section of our development group. We take ideas and make them into products. For example, we're working on a whole range of health and fitness incentives for individuals and corporations. If our customers stay fit—they save us money. What are you up to now, Tom?"

"I'm a consultant—helping to put together and facilitate programs like that".

They swapped numbers and got ready to start the warm-up'

Sam and Suzi's Race Warm-Up

1. Walk slowly for 5 minutes
2. Walk faster for 5 minutes
3. Walk and jog for 5 minutes
4. Line up for the race.

Tom excused himself from the Sam & Suzi warm-up when he saw Chris. They chatted—and ran the slow part of the warmup together. Chris was not very open about how he felt about his new workout group—but Tom read that as pre-race nervousness. When they started the accelerations, Tom wanted to do them on the last mile of the course—whereas Chris had a new routine—and took off. He zoomed through these high speed accelerations, while Tom did his 40-year-old gentle accelerations, and got a preview of the last mile—a tough one.

As the race started Sam told Suzi that he wanted to do one of these a week to keep the motivation going. "Once I get here I feel supported, bouyed up by the energy. There's no way I can't do this 5K," said Sam.

Meanwhile Chris took off with the lead group, composed of many of his workout partners, most of whom were the fastest runners in the Atlanta area. The one star who was not in the group took the lead: Tim Kennedy. Tim was Atlanta's best chance for placing someone in the Olympics—and had raced internationally. Chris and Tim had also been competitors about 10 years ago—when Chris was part of a children's track program—and Tim was a soccer player.

Since his legs felt tight, Chris hung back—the last racer in the lead pack—which stayed together until the mile and a quarter mark. As they started up a 400 meter hill, Tim took off. Chris couldn't believe that no one wanted to go with him and so he instinctively passed the others and stalked Tim. As

they crested the hill, Tim still had a 30 yard lead on Chris—who glided into position behind him—using the technique Tom showed him. The race was on.

Tom stayed back in the second pack until just before the crest of the hill. When he saw the lead pack breaking up, he started picking off one after another. Tom felt that he was right on the edge of his physical limits—but he made the decision to go—and learn from the experience. Tom's game was to use his coasting muscles to stay right behind each succive competitor, and then use downhills to go by them, coasting up the the next person. He was having fun.

Suzi and Sam walked and jogged pleasantly until the half-way hill. Sam not only had no trouble with it—he jogged the last part of it. It was all Suzi could do to keep up with him. "I guess my hill work paid off—didn't it." said Sam.

With one mile to go, Chris passed by his new coach who was cheering on the curb—just as they turned. The coach got a little too excited when he saw Chris closing in on Tim. None of his athletes had ever beaten Tim and the coach was screaming with excitement "Pass him NOW, Chris—DO IT!" Chris hesitated, because he had been following Tom's advice to "stalk his prey", holding back his acceleration power until the finish line came into view. But as soon as the coach's order had sunk in, Chris accelerated.

In a wave of anxiety and power, Chris made up 30 meters and then zoomed by Tim, who smoothly tucked in behind him. The length of a football field later, Chris was gritting his teeth, trying to hang on as Tim smoothly moved alongside. Then, as if his legs just forgot how to run, it was over for Chris. His main driving muscles turned to jelly and wouldn't work. He went into slow motion, and felt numb all over. His breathing went from a heavy but deep motion—to shallow and out of control.

Up the first hill, Tom passed two runners. Going down the other side he built up momentum and used it effectively passing three more on the second hill. Cresting that one, he saw the finish line—at the top of the final hill—but with another dip to build momentum. One after another, Tom picked off the competitors, 15 and 20 years younger than he—and he did it by using his turnover and smoothness—without driving the muscles into over-fatigue.

But as Tom moved up the final hill, about 400 meters long, he realized that he had gone just a bit too fast. His legs got tight and slowed down. Most of the runners he had passed in the last mile, passed him back. Feeling worse and worse about his performance he passed one runner who was moving more slowly—and suddenly realized it was a struggling Chris. He slowed down and ran in the last 20 meters with his son, finishing in 15:59. As father and son struggled to exit the finish chute, Tom realized that the runner who had snuck in just ahead of him at the finish line was Dr. Lifowitz.

Sam had to wait for Suzi on two of the hills, as they walked for 2 minutes and ran for 2 minutes. Sam had, indeed, found some strength in his uphill legs, and was on a runner's high, as he philosophized:

Afterward, Tom joined the duo. Sam was feeling good again. "I couldn't have done this without you who are my 'tribe'. As we came toward the finish—I had this overwhelming sense that you were surrounding me pulling me with psychic energy. The power and the satisfaction of that experience is difficult to describe."

Tom said he wasn't sure the energy was coming from him—he had spent it all in the last mile of the race. When the others asked him how his race went, Tom said that he had gotten too carried away trying to beat the 20 year-olds in the race. His left brain was driving him to pass one and then another, and he gave in to the ego boost. His greatest regret, was not being able to talk to Chris—who snuck off after the race.

"You guys would be proud of Dr. Life— he passed both me and Chris at the finish line. That guy's amazing. He can go for several nights without sleep—and run at his top form. I'm going to study the handout sheet he gave me."

As the trio drove home, they shared the many positive reinforcements of the day. Tom mentioned that the fellow he met in the insurance business wanted to get his ideas about incentives for health insurance—no chance of a job—but an opportunity to break into the industry.

Suzi had the only negative observation. She overheard Chris's new coach berating him in front of the other athletes. The critical barbs hurled at Chris sent the message that the coach thought he was not mentally tough enough to maintain his strong finish against Tim. Coach Masimi didn't expect anything out of Chris if he didn't change the mushy way he ran. Just as he was saying this, Tim, the winner, came by and told Chris that he had run a courageous race and may have won if he had waited a little longer.

"Oh, Tom, there was one other bit of news which only makes sense to you— let's see if I can remember it...somebody told me that last week on a hard course, Dylan ran 15:01."

Tom glossed over that to ask how Sam had done—and Suzi explained how hard it was for her to keep up with him, Tom was impressed:

"Sam, you're the real champion today— think how far you've come since we met—before the trip back from Boston."

"I'm thinking how far I've come in the last 14 days. It was 2 weeks ago when I was sitting in the hospital not wanting to live. I'm now hoping that your friend 'crazy Jim' can come up with a real reason for me to fight the University over my beloved grant."

They talked candidly about their emotions—starting first with Suzi who was mad at Sam when she realized what he had done. "We've invested something more important than money in you—our personal energy and support—we believe in you, and you almost let us down...I'm speaking totally

as a person now—and not as a psychologist."

Sam thought for a few moments and then related how his problems and exercise had become intertwined. "That was a small part of my problem—I hadn't exercised in 10 days, was losing my focus and realized that I was letting you good people down—because you believed in me. But it was so much more comprehensive than that...I was letting down my profession, my family, my whole life was crumbling—and I didn't think I had anythiing to replace it with....but I really did."

"You see, I had withdrawn inside my shell, when actually you folks, my wife and family and several other key friends were in full support of me. I just couldn't reach out and connect. Most dissappointing was my refusal to do the one thing that brings back my good attitude and my tribal instincts....exercise."

I couldn't articluate this before—but even on the really bad days, when there seemed no options, an exercise session with you two would turn it around. I felt better about myself, from somewhere there was hope—no specific answers— just hope. But when I got a continuous stream of bad news at work it affected my family life and I chose to do nothing."

"It may be that I won't ever return to teach the area I dearly love—and that my economic life continues to go downhill—but I'm going to finish that Peachtree Road Race. And at the very least, I feel that I will keep trying to turn things around at work—and at home."

They had been parked alongside the curb at Suzi's place for several minutes—and neither of the three had realized it. Suzi told the stories of 2 of her clients who had gone through a series of terrible lifestyle changes—and had only made progress when they started to exercise regularly. She also said that most of those who experienced similar problems who didn't exercise—didn't make any significant, long term changes.

They walked to a nearby hill where the finish line of the Peachtree was visible. Sam said what each was thinking: There, at that orange-painted stripe is our future—and it is ours.

And for that moment, each felt focused, and the problems which had weighted them down a few hours ago evaporated. They toasted their exuberance with a PowerBar which Tom tore into three pieces.

Under the glow of the carbohydrate, the endorphins, and the compadarie, Suzi said:

"I used to think that runners were preoccupied with the way they looked and some wierd negative avoidance of future disease or something. Now, all I see is the positive. It only takes a short run to unleash a lot of positive things inside—making you feel like really DOING something. The face of a runner may seem serious and focused on the outside—but we're smiling inside."

Tom knew that it was Chris at the other end of the phone. While he was only starting to get to know his adult son, he instinctively realized that it was a major step in their relationship for him to call—with that tone in his voice.

As father and son made their way down the first mile of the Kennesaw trail, nothing was said—but then the terrain offered a series of small ups and downs. This was good for Chris, who had a tendency to feel great for the first 10 minutes, go too fast, and then suffer during the rest of the run because of it. Running slower allowed Chris to notice that the south side the mountain looked like a lumpy green fur-ball. Once he adapted to the reality that he had to adjust for terrain, the son enjoyed the natural, primitive environment; he told Tom that he could imagine being the first explorer who found this native trail hiway.

Tom started the confessional, by saying that he wasn't so sure that he was going to be very competitive against Dylan at Peachtree—because of his poor perfor- mance at the Home Depot 5K. Chris didn't say anything for a while as Tom

spun out a series of excuses about mo- mentum lost during his layoff from running, old legs, old injuries, etc. While he was saying this, Tom felt that Chris was getting ready to say something—and he did.

But Chris waited for a few moments of absolute silence as both enjoyed the natural coziness of the trail system. Most of the course was thickly forested, with a variety of pine forests, bridges over creeks, and stretches along the original earthworks used during what Sam's grandfather called "The War of Southern Independence." At regular intervals they would break into a clearing with a vista over a field. While there were houses near the trail, one could run practically all of the 16 mile loop without seeing them.

Just when Tom thought he needed to ask a question to keep things going, Chris started unwinding.

"From the time I was little I always thought that you were better than the other fathers—regardless of whether you were around or not—because you pursued your dream. Mom told me many times about how you believed so much in your chance to make the Olympic team that you made great sacrifices. I think that she still resents that—but I don't. That story told me over and over that my old man stood for something—and that I was made of that same stuff."

So many people today have their schemes for making money, for having a great lifestyle with a 'status' car, house, and vacation retreat—but that stuff doesn't compute with me. You were right to do what you could do to make that 1980 Olympic team—to see what you're made of. I want to become part of a dream, and that's why I'm here. I just don't know what dream I should be a part of."

"You don't need a dream," said Tom, "you need a belief environment—which produces visions."

Tom couldn't believe that this was coming out of his mouth. He was responding to his son with the most honest advice he could give; the ideas were pouring out of him before he could think about them. Indeed, Suzi had helped him greatly by dragging him away from the NCAA final four tournament. But he conveyed it to his son with conviction. Not only did he feel that he was helping Chris to project his vision beyond Peachtree—into next year and beyond. He was explaining how he had been subconsciously constructing his belief environment for himself.

"So you're not ready to give up your pursuit of Dylan at Peachtree", asked Chris.

"Hell No!" said Tom. That earlier statement was my reaction to a momentary setback—which will only make me tougher and more capable.

"I still may not beat Dylan—but I'll be stronger inside than he."

They both ran in silence for a while, passing the Kolb farmhouse—a relic left over from one of the battles of Kennesaw Mountain. As they ran along the sides of an interesting ravine leading down to a creek, Chris opened up some more.

"I still think that Masimi is a good coach—but things just weren't right—I wasn't having fun."

Tom thought for several strides, then asked: "What do you want to do?"

"I don't know....a first step would be a good Peachtree. Everything has turned out to be so different that what I thought—Atlanta isn't an easy-going southern town—it's a very busy city and everybody's working—all the time. I thought I could make a name for myself by running Peachtree—but no one cares who wins."

"What do you mean..."

"With 50,000 people signing up in one day—I would have thought that the town would worship the winner. But these...Peachtreers...are just in it for themselves—for their own experience."

"At first I resented this—as if they were taking something away from my potential for recognition and accomplishment.

Then I realized that they were right. Just over-hearing what Suzi and Sam are getting out of the training experience—I realize that there are so many more important things going on. And when I see you helping them—you are my hero, again.

There was nothing more that needed to be said on that run. After thousands of runs which were faster, and built better racing skills—this was the run that Tom will remember for the rest of his life.

et's go!

And with that Shout, Tom took the lead down a long hill on the north side of Dallas hiway. Chris seemed to enjoy the challenge of staying light on his feet through patches of gravel—and then found that the light touch was simply a good tactic in any terrain. Tom flew across a bouncy wooden bridge, gaining a 20 meter lead on Chris—who accepted the challenge. Even as Tom used his craft to accelerate up the next hill without using up the muscle power in his legs, Chris was stalking him.

Over the crest, Tom took off, more efficient and smooth than at any time in his life. Chris enjoyed being patient in this performance game—he was having fun accelerating for 40-80 meters and then gliding for at least that amount. After one mile which took them to a crossing of Burnt Hickory Road, they took a break, laughed, and then took off on some more accelerations on the other side—playing a version of fox and hounds—only they were so intuitively into the chase that it was more a real animal version than a child's version. Chris got into it so much that he didn't realize that they had returned to the

visitor's center.

When Chris promised to be "good and listen to his father" Tom said he would show him a neat surprise—and they ran (at 9 minute per mile pace) up the trails to the top of Kennesaw Mountain. It was a beautiful day and both just looked at the geography, at the great view of the Atlanta skyline, and at Stone Mountain— which was clearly visible on this low humidity—low haze day.

As they decended, about one minute per mile faster than the ascent, Chris told how he wanted to get caught up in the Olympic excitement the following year, and that he hoped that the two of them could train together. The ride home was spent in plotting strategy, setting up a racing schedule, and then looking beyond Peachtree.

Tom talked Chris through the concepts he had received from Suzi in the Galloway Guerrilla Guide. Since Chris was not taking classes during the summer, and Tom was not working, they both agreed to try the 3 a day workout program from GGG.

Chris, speaking in a comfortable and

confident tone, asked Tom what he was going to do for work.

"I've got a little money saved up, Chris, and I'm really going to start my own business. I've been telling that to other people for weeks now—but only after this run did I really feel it slipping securely into my belief

environment.....But the force of my life for the next 3 weeks is Peachtree—to run the race of my life."

Me too, said Chris." and when he saw the fire in his father's eyes—Chris knew he had a training partner—if he could stay up with him.

I thought that this would be a good choice for a restaurant—because they give you lots of room on the table, said Suzi, as she spread out the contents of her Galloway Guerilla Guide.

"I don't think that you're told us the whole story, said Tom."

Suzi thought a minute and came up with another rationalization: "OK this is located right on the Peachtree course—

and we can get to know it better....Not good enough ...Somebody who works here runs?..."

"OK...True confessions...They have positively, absolutely, the best cheesecake in town."

So on an honest note the evening started, as Sam and his wife filed in, followed by Chris and a female non-running college friend. Sam volunteered to be the fat gram police—and Suzi replied that if he

**Peachtree Countdown Schedule for Tom and Chris
(3 workouts per day)**

Mon	Tue	Wed	Thu	Fri	Sat	Sun
1)Easy 5-7mi	very easy 8-10 mi	Easy 5-7	Strength	Easy 5-7	5K race	H2Orun
2)2-4mi of accelerations	H2O run	3-4 mi of accelerations	H20 run	2-4 mi of accelerations	6-8 mi very easy	swim
3)speed play on roads, 4-6mi	1-2 mi light accelerations	track play 4-6mi	H2O run swim	3-4 mi easy cross country	2-4mi light accelerations	hike or walk

really wanted to assume that role, there was a table for him across the room.

After a while the conversation naturally broke off into two groups. Sam's wife was from the same home town as Chris's friend, Fort Walton Beach, Florida. They talked about many families, places, events—and even a church—which they had shared in common.

Chris and Tom were plotting their training for the 3 weeks leading up to Peachtree—and then beyond. But they needed their interpreter, Suzi, to explain some of the concepts in GGG. She had gone an extra step—talked to Jeff Galloway and had received a conceptual schedule from him.

"The concept of higher weekly mileage definitely helps improve conditioning—Galloway said in the GGG—but at great risk" noted Suzi.. "He offered this to those who want to achieve at a higher level, but need to lower the chance of injury which comes with increased intensity."

"But after two weeks of good work, we'll need to ease off on the work—to freshen up the legs, said Tom.

"So we're breaking up the work into smaller components, allowing for recovery between, and enforcing two non-running days" added Chris.

"You must take those days off from running—or you compromise the program," said Suzi. "But you can get some great workouts in the water."

Chris thought that water running was an activity only for injured runners. Tom set him straight on that—telling him that the great pool workouts he did one month ago, kept him from losing any conditioning during his two week layoff. Tom said that he had read that Mary Decker Slaney had actually set an American record—just 3 days out of several weeks in the water.

"Wow, Mary Slaney did that? This stuff must work!" said Chris excitedly.

When the waiter came to ask about dessert—Suzi was ready.

"I'm buying!" she commanded, "to celebrate my loss of 10 pounds!...even better...3 dress sizes!"

Sam's wife asked Suzi for her secret formula, and Chris's friend told Suzi that she was going in just the opposite direction—while eating less. They were both impressed with her symbolic eating of cheesecake. "You gotta get on the Peachtree fat-burning program," affirmed Suzi as she put a big bite of cheesecake on her fork.

Everyone enjoyed the dessert—even some of the fat-free flavors.

"When I started this exercise thing I promised myself that I wouldn't starve myself—that I would stay focused on finishing the Peachtree and not deprive myself of energy supply— and I haven't. She took another big bite of the chocolate piece.

I want you to know that I have had at least one slice of cheesecake—at least once a week throughout the campaign. I still love it—but in small doses.

With forks hoisted in a "toast", Suzi said "on to Peachtree". The quartet agreed to meet at Lenox Square to do the course again on Saturday at 9:30. Sam's wife, Bonnie, had been nudging Sam to leave in order to pick up their kids—for 30 minutes. But having heard of Suzi's success against the scales, she stayed for another 20 minutes learning about the starvation reflex, teaching the muscles to become fat burners, etc. Bonnie and Chris's friend (Sally) agreed to join Sam and Suzi to at least start their program on Saturday morning.

As they were waiting for the check, every person at the table made a positive and confident statement about how they were going to feel after finishing Peachtree. But then, each admitted that there were doubts, anxieties, and currents of insecurity which intermingled. Suzi told them that there was a final mental training session at Phidippides on Sunday afternoon—which would be taught by Jeff Galloway. There was general agreement that the mental area was the most important as the clock ticked down toward July 4th.

...and the strength of an invisible rubber band

Galloway was comfortably chatting with some of the folks in the audience when the leader of his marathon program advised that it was time to get started. Jeff started the talk asking for the concerns, motivational problems and general information which the various members of the audience would like to hear about and discuss. A few were still having trouble getting motivated to start a program, but Sam wanted help to stay committed, Chris and Tom needed a boost to break through personal barriers, and Suzi asked about the series of anxieties which continue to bother most of those who work toward lifestyle change goals. As the speaker launched into his presentation, he offered techniques and suggestions which could help each person with his or her area of interest.

The War

It's natural to feel anxieties, doubts, and insecurities when you challenge yourself—the negatives are part of the process. When under stress, the two sides of your brain go to war. If you've programmed yourself to deal with the problems, you'll tend to stay in the right brain. This creative and intuitive center will help to steer you in the direction of your potential. We'll talk about how the programming works in a few minutes.

The left side of the brain is programmed to be negative—when you're under stress. You might call it the 'lazy brain'. It has a million excuses why you should slow down, stop, avoid discomfort—or just not get out there in the first place. Through mental training, you can minimize the time in the left brain, and find by-passes around it. The problems, in themselves, are not usually the reason for goal frustration and motivation shifts. You slow down because you become preoccupied with the problems, listen too much to the left brain, and let it get you down. The strength is inside you, let's work on pulling it out.

The Training

These three mental training techniques will certainly give you confidence to overcome the negative stream of thoughts from the left side. A greater goal, however, is to develop a plan of action, rehearsed in advance many times, which helps you to react quickly. Just the acts of having a plan and taking action will bestow confidence and improve attitude.

By anticipating the problems in advance, and having these three strategies ready to work—you will be setting up a process which leads to the solution—step by step. Incredible capabilities and solutions are available to you through practice. Just as you must workout your muscles, mental training must be done several times a week—if you want to improve in that area. The regular use of these mental training techniques will keep these procedures 'in shape'.

Mental Rehearsal

Go through the anticipated experience in advance many times in a positive but realistic way. You must anticipate every possible problem which could occur during the experience—but move through the problems to the next part of the experience. As you rehearse these challenges over and over, you'll gain a clearer vision of what is possible, how to do it, and will take action during the experience itself..

A primary benefit of the rehearsal is to desensitize you to the problems which may occur in the exerience itself. It's to your advantage to over-rehearse the number of problems and the intensity of each. In this way, you will be over-prepared for the difficulties—and a lessened version is unlikely to cause an over-reaction from the left brain. Remember, it's not the problem that causes you to slow down—it's your believing in those negative left brain messages. Your mental training can help you stay under the control of the right brain, which can

intuitively steer you to what is possible.

In the case of Peachtree, start your rehearsal with your July 4th wake-up.

Concepts of Mental Rehearsal

1. Control your environment—feel secure, positive, not stressed
2. Lower the anticipated effort of the exercise—make it easily do-able
3. Manipulate the variables in the rehearsal so that you feel confident about your effort
4. Break down the experience into a series of steps—each of which is easy
5. Build in mental 'pats on the back' throughout the rehearsal
6. Over time, anticipate every possible problem you could encounter—and get through each
7. It helps to rehearse problems which are more difficult than you will encounter—so that the actual ones are not as difficult.
8. Be realistic and positive throughout your rehearsal
9. By going out slowly (staying within yourself) in challenges of any type, you are more likely to stay under the positive direction of the rehearsal.
10. Be sure to include some fun, and some positive reinforcement in your rehearsal.

Mentally work through all of the nervous feelings, and go through each of the preparation steps for the day: drink 4-6 oz of water every 30 minutes, etc. As you mentally run the race from start to finish, deal with the problems such as starting to run through an early water stop—when you should be walking and drinking. In many cases, you'll mentally push through problems by 'digging down a little deeper' and going on. Some folks start the rehearsal by writing down the basic 'plot outline'. As the days or weeks go by in your rehearsing, the 'plot' becomes more sophistocated, realistic and effective. It's better, however, to teach yourself to rehearse without use of pencil and paper.

You can use this rehearsal technique to anticipate problems in a business meeting, and to steer the progress of the meeting in certain directions. When you have communication problems with others, you can get a clearer concept of the issues, and then work out every possible solution through this process.

**Mental Rehearsal:
Getting out the Door—at the end of a hard day**

1. Tell yourself that you're not going to work out—take the pressure off.
2. Rehearse putting on exercise clothes, and shoes, as soon as you get home—just to be comfortable.
3. Walk around the house, listening to upbeat music, have a cup of tea, PowerBar, etc
4. Tell yourself that you're just going to go outside the front door to see what the weather is like.
5. Once outside you"ll walk to the end of the block—to see what the neighbors are doing.
6. You decide to walk across the street
7. You're on your way!

Magic Words

A second line of mental offence and defense is part of a complex mental programming network in which a few key words can trigger a stream from your positive past. The magic comes not from the words themselves—but from the association of your experiences with the words. When you connect a word with an experience during which you've solved a problem, you help the right brain find the same intuitive path to a future solution.

I have three words which counterattack three problems associated with fatigue. 'Relax' confronts the tendency to tighten up at the end of a hard workout. Since my tendency is to push the muscles too hard when they are tired—I need to relax. 'Power' attacks the tendency to lose strength at the end of a hard or long effort. 'Glide' helps me get my running form to become smoother when I start to run ragged.

Over the years, I've directly associated hundreds of experiences with these three words. In each experience, my performance started to drop off—and I got it back together. Sometimes I got on with the challenge and recorded a lifetime best. In most cases, however, I was able to do as well as I could do on that day. In either case, the words performed their magic because they directly engaged an experience recall.

The sensation is that your memory bank is flooding into your consciousness with experience after experience—all positive. This keeps the left brain from inserting its negative messages, for an extended period of time. I've also noticed that on many occasions, the process extends further than this. Somehow, connections are made to inner sources of strength which help to solve the problems as they have been solved in the past. Other 'switches' are turned on which bestow confidence and a positive attitude—based on the overwhelming successful pattern of your experience inventory. The more experiences you have directly associated with the words, the more powerful the words will be.

Magic Words

1. To help you through problems, articulate the major areas where you break down mentally.
2. Give each problem a positive, magic word which counters that problem.
3. Go back through your memory bank and bring back the experiences where you have been successful—when you started to lose focus due to those problems.
4. Attach the magic word or words to those experiences. As you review the success in your mind, keep saying the magic word over and over again.
5. Keep adding experiences to your magic word inventory—in workouts, races, or other challenges.
6. The more experiences you have associated with your words, the more magical they are.
7. When the positive control of the mental rehearsal starts to wear out, start using the magic words.
8. Say the words over and over.
9. It helps to practice recalling the words and experiences during enjoyable exercise sessions—as well as the challenging ones.

Dirty Tricks

...including the 'giant, invisble rubber band'

If the exercise continues to get difficult, there will come a time when the rehearsal loses its positive control and the words don't have much magic. Now is the time for a few 'dirty tricks'.

I carry with me, in all of my races, a bag of these which help to activate the creative part of the brain—the right side. This is a collection of thoughts, sayings, mental images—all of which are just strange enough that the logical or left side doesn't know what to do with them. One of them is the giant, invisible rubber band.

It is mounted behind me in the small of my back. Late in the race, when there's no more magic in the magic words, and somebody passes me, my left brain goes wild: "look how good he/she looks—and how bad you feel", or "It's over", "Slow down—it's not worth it".

At that point, I lasso the passer with my giant rubber band—but he/she doesn't realize it because it's invisible. For a while, this faster runner will continue to get ahead of me, but I will imagine how the tension is building on the rubber band, around the chest—or even better, around the neck (cutting off oxygen supply to the brain). Just by using this imagination process I'm able to get out of my misery and distract the left brain for 100-800 meters.

But at some point, I laugh at myself for believing in such a 'hokey' trick. One of the great benefits of laughing, is that it helps you get into the right brain, and it helps you relax. This often triggers a chain reaction:

1. My stride length shortens, which loosens the leg muscles.
2. This enables the legs to turnover faster, increasing rhythm and speed.
3. I catch up with, or pass, the person who passed me.

There is always more strength and ability inside us—but we give in to the left brain too easily when it sends us messages to ease off. By starting the creative process, we get into the right brain—which can intuitively search for our potential on that day.

Our right brain has an unlimited number of creative solutions to any problem. With the use of these three stategies, you can have your best opportunity to stay close to its control—and do what you're capable of doing on that day.

Chris was so motivated after the session that he had to call Tom. Because he had been dozing to the background noise of ESPN, Tom's answer to this phone wake-up call (at 11pm) had an irritating tone. Chris applologized for calling—but when Tom found out that he wanted to talk about his training—he invited him over. There was a full refrigerator of fruit juice, diet drinks, and gatorade, which stayed open all night.

Chris had his schedule for the next week—but they went beyond that,

constructing a 5 year plan—with all the workouts "penciled in". Then they plotted Peachtree strategy. At 2:50am, Chris crashed on the couch, and the old man finally got his rest. "I'm ready to 'relax, glide and power-sleep'," he said.

Used to getting up at 6, Tom couldn't get back to sleep—and Chris awoke to the smell of coffee just before 7 on Monday morning. While he didn't have any appointments, Tom had used every day to work out networking strategies, make phone calls, and prepare outlines for proposals. He had 3 meetings during the next 3 days, which Tom called "fishing expeditions". Knowing that he wouldn't get any business, Tom was looking for these more relaxed sessions to see what was out there—and to work on his presentation skills.

As they munched on PowerBars, father and son talked about a route in the Sandy Springs area, and decided to use the relatively flat terrain of Mt. Vernon Hiway. Tom enjoyed a good strong cup of coffee, while Chris opted for gatorade—although he wasn't so sure about the combination of the sports bar and the sports drink.

Just before they headed out the door at 8am, the phone rang. Bill Stearns, the insurance exec Tom had met at the Home Depot 5K was on the line, asking Tom to come in and chat about his ideas on prevention programs—and the managed approach to health care. Tom set up a time between the morning slow run, and the mid-day acceleration session.

"In four months, we've come to know one another pretty well," said Tom, as they munched on fat-free saltines and salsa at Sam's house.

"Maybe too well," added Sam, as everyone chuckled.

Suzi was proud to know that she would finish the Peachtree and hoped she could be wearing the shirt when she saw Dylan. Sam admitted he still had some butterflies and wanted to go over some of the main areas of concern. Suzi referred to

the GGG at regular intervals.

Sam had been eating PowerBars all afternoon, and was pretty sick of them. He was looking for something else low in fat and low in salt, which would give a little feeling of satisfaction. Suzi went out to her car for her surprise, fat-free cheesecake.

Tom brought in some bagles which he cut up and used to dip for some extra hot sauce which he had found in Texas. He had this carbohydrate source all to himself.

Timetable: July 4th
5am: Wake Up

5-5:30:	Drink 6-8 oz of water and eat one half of a PowerBar	7:30:	Start (Chris and Tom) Suzi and Sam start walking
5:50:	Meet at Phidippides to carpool to Marta (bring throw-away water bottle)	8:00:	Start (Sam and Suzi) approximately (drink 6-8 oz of water)
		8:00:30	(approximately) Chris and Tom finish
6:05:	Board MARTA train for Lenox Station (drink 6-8 oz of water)	9:00:	Sam and Suzi finish (approximately) (drink 6-8oz of water)
6:20-6:45:	arrive in Lenox parking lot (use porto-johns as needed)	9:15:	Gather on the west side of the stage—at designated tree
6:50-7:10:	get into respective staging area (drink 6-8 oz of water)	10:00	After awards—Party at Suzi's

Chris arrived with a great fruit salad, which was the hit of the party, along with Sam's fat-free pound cake.

"Fat-free pound cake?" questioned Suzi, who thought it a contradiction in terms. But it tasted quite good with the fruit. The recipe used fat-free cream cheese.

As the quartet gave their last toasts (with diet sprite) they asked Suzi for some last minute mental boosts, which she had already copied for each to take home:

Mental Performance Pushers

* I feel confident and relaxed

* I see myself walking and running with confidence

* This is a good day

* I'm feeling great energy flow from the center of my body to the legs and arms

* Momentary lapses in concentration and energy are followed by increased flow and confidence

* I am successful—I am part of the process of success

Sam knew how many of his students must feel at the end of a challenging semester. He was about to take the final exam, and he couldn't sleep all night. At first he was annoyed, then frustrated. But when anger entered the emotional scene, he reached for GALLOWAY'S BOOK ON RUNNING and was reassured that it's OK to lose sleep the night before a race; often the best performances come under those circumstances.

The quartet had decided to rendezvous at Phidippides and carpool to the Arts Center Marta Station. There was a stream of headlights at 5:30 on every major traffic artery in town leading to Lenox. All of the major Marta Stations were jammed as many of the over 50,000 participants were being dropped off. It was exciting to become part of a great tide of energy flowing positively in one direction. They joined the flow of thousands into Lenox Square and participated in the ancient 'porto-john' ritual. Leaving Lenox, they looked toward the intersection of Peachtree and Lenox Rd to an unbelieveable scene of runners everywhere.

"The migration of the tribes has started," said Sam.

Suzi and Sam walked Chris and Tom to their start position, which helped Sam reduce his nervousness. Suzi was excitedly optimistic, Sam was upbeat and solid as the competitors parted from their support crew. "You are our warriors going into battle," said Sam. "You will win and bring us honor."

Sam and Suzi walked back to the last group, outside the fenced area near the sidewalk. First, they passed by the competitive (seeded) groups, which seemed more quiet and focused. Each group was in a party mood. By the time they reached the end, Sam realized that they were part of a moving celebration— a celebration of the positives. Hearing a familiar voice, Sam turned and saw his department head walk by. Their eyes met and Sam merely said "Hi". Dr. Palmer said in passing, "I hope you're not getting yourself in over your head." He quickly excused himself, saying that he had learned how to get a better position, "two groups up."

Tom and Chris didn't talk much as they moved into position and waited for the start. The sight behind them was inspiring and amazing: tens of thousands of Peachtree-ers, all propelled by nervous energy.

As Tom looked on the starting line he tried to take away the butterflies in his stomach which he brought with him from over 25 years of competition. It was as if he was suddenly alone in a survival trek against a hoard of barbarians.

But as he looked ahead at Chris, who was talking to a young man his age, he became grounded. As if Suzi was there calming him down and going through the relaxation exercises. That whole experience came back as Tom thought of the positive effect of being together. He looked at Chris and suddenly realized how lucky he was to be a fatherand that he could share this experience with his son. This was a migration—of values, positive mental energy, and dedication—from one generation to another. For the first time since he had entered his first road race, the first Peachtree, 25 years ago, Tom was secure. Now, he was migrating with the tribes, instead of against them.

But he was still nervous as the national anthem was sung, and the press truck moved into position in front of the elite athletes. As the gun fired, Tom felt the support of Chris, but when he looked ahead and went with the tremendous flow of human energy, he felt the presence of only one person—Dylan.

Everything went according to plan for the first mile. Tom and Chris made their way to the front of the sub-seeded pack.

They focused on the back of the elite runners as they weaved through groups of mostly young runners who went out too fast, and were already slowing down.

"I hate to say it, but those guys are in for a bad time", said Chris. "I know because I've been there!"

As they made the turn where Roswell Road joined Peachtree, Tom felt the elevation drop very slightly. Chris instinctively let his stride out a notch, and started to pull away from Tom, who said two words of warning, "too long." Chris adjusted, and was immediately running lighter on his feet.

Tom knew that Chris was a great downhill runner, and told him to take off. But, between breaths, he blurted, "light and short."

Chris realized that this was his day. He felt strong and the switch was on. Without feeling any effort, he moved quickly past clumps of runners in the back of the elite pack. By the time he passed Second Ponce de Leon Baptist Church, he was clicking off one runner after another in a line.

As he passed the bridge over Peachtree Creek, Chris made his only mistake of this race. He saw his friend Tim, about 60 meters ahead, and decided to catch him by the top of Piedmont Hospital hill. He let the left brain drive him up the hill.

Tom was flowing very smoothly and very well down the hill, passing runners in groups of 3 and 4. As he crossed over the Peachtree Creek bridge he again felt the negative presence of someone, and out of the corner of his eyehe realized it was Dylan. The long-haired runner moved over toward the curb to take advantage of a tangent in the road, and bumped into Tom. Tom moved over.

"Surprise, surprise, Burke. I didn't think you had it in you."

Then Dylan bumped Tom again, this time forcing him up on the curb. Tom wanted to retaliate in the most emotional way, but the belief environment and vision he had been growing, connecting and nuturing for months prevailed. He dropped back slightly and tucked in behind Dylan.

Meanwhile, the pack had slowly walked toward the start. Sam struck up a conversation with a fellow who was taking some courier envelopes to friends in Mid-town. "It started as a joke, and has gotten more elaborate. I don't try to bring chocolate anymore It melted and oozed out last year."

The race continued to go well for Chris. He smoothly moved by one competitor, then another, and then a third, as the Piedmont Hospital hill started to take it's toll. Making the final push, he counted three competitors between him and Tim Kennedy. Passing Shephard Spinal Center, the elevation seemed to get much tougher, but so did Chris. For just a moment, the 21 year old lost his focus on the finish line in Piedmont Park and decided to conquer this hill. His exhilaration empowered him to move with strength past a Kenyan, then an Australian, and finally an Alabamian as he crested the top, tucking in behind Tim.

All of the athletes were feeling the effort, and the humidity. Chris was tired from his effort, but he was bouyed up by passing other athletes. Instincts were good, however, and Tim welcomed him. "Lets go after each one of them, Chris." Let's work together."

The gentle uphilll stretch between I-85 and Colony Square seemed almost too easy for Chris, but he wisely followed Tim's conservative tactics. But just as Chris thought he had the chance to really compete with Tim, the effort started to get very hard as they crested Colony Square. Tim was moving away from him and Chris knew that he was in trouble competitively.

As the Kenyan passed him, Chris summoned all of the courage he had, and used the downhill on 14th Street to catch up with Tim. As they entered the Park, there were two Europeans just ahead and Tim smoothly went by them. With what seemed like his last effort, Chris passed the Kenyan, and struggled to hang on to Italy's 3rd best 10K runner, but he felt Tim moving ahead of him, and there was no bounce left in his legs. For a moment, on a little downhill above the soccer fields, Chris thought that he might be able to hang on in this position and gut it out, but the leg muscles were spent. The harder he tried, the tighter Chris got. The Kenyan passed him back, and when the Italian went by, Chris started to fade into a lactic-acid oblivion compounded by the racer's enemy from within, negative left brain messages which said, "slow down, give up, it's over."

Tom was not feeling very good either,

which turned out to be a blessing His 42 year-old legs seemed tight, and he knew there would be possible sites of cramping with any un-smart move. This conservative "governor" kept him running smoothly in a group of 15 or so as they moved up the long hill towards Piedmont Hospital. As the large group started to string out, Tom moved instinctivly to the outside. By the time he passed the Shepherd Spinal Center, he had passed his original pack and was working his way up through another 20+ person group, led by Dylan..

As Tom watched others grimace, he smiled inside, shortened his stride a hair, and made sure that each step was light and smooth. Starting up the final stretch and Piedmont Hospital, Tom resisted the temptation to go after a runner who passed him. "Conserve,.Conserve, Conserve," he said, as he held back going over the crest. Just for an instant, he got a quick glimpse of Dylan, interwined in a pack of runners about 40 meters ahead.

Tom no longer cared about Dylan. He was stalking prey just ahead. His leg seemed to relax as he passed over I-85 and he smoothly moved by one group, and then worked through another. On 4 occasions his legs started to tighten up and lose power as he passed WSB Studios, then the Woodruff Art Center and then Colony Square. Each time, Tom backed off the effort and shortened the stride. To his surprise, his rhythm picked up, then the speed, and he gained confidence and motivation passing 2-3 runners at a time. He instinctively shifted gears over and over again, just has he had in his workouts.

Two competitors in the masters division came back after him as they moved downhill on 14th Street, but Tom was having fun. Passing under the arch into Piedmont Park, he realized that he was passing Dylan, whose form was deteriorating due to fatigue. Again, Dylan angled over and tried to bump Tom. While he missed, Dylan's hand hit Tom's trailing foot, knocking him off balance.

The next 4 seconds seemed like an eternity to Tom who thought that he was going to end up skidding on his chest down the road along the Tennis Center. Somehow, he instinctively corrected himself—while the adrenalyn was flowing through his body.

The tactic worked for Dylan in the short run. While Tom struggled to get his balance, heading off course toward the Tennis center, Dylan lengthened his stride and got 30 meters on his adversary. But Tom was mad and the adrenalin rush was moblizing his physical resources and his mental focus was as intense as a laser. As Tom's stride moved into the mechanical efficiency he had developed each running day during the last 2 months, all of his resources turned toward the finish line, focused on one competitor at a time.

Tom didn't notice the pain in his foot or the blister on each toe of his other foot. He was running with the heart, and his whole being was mobilizing the resources to move with whatever energy was left and it kept on coming. As he instinctively made his stride quieter, Tom's speed picked up a notch. He was breathing hard and deep, pulling strength out of each breath.

While his legs didn't want to respond coming off the hill, Tom abstractly realized that Dylan was no more than 20 meters ahead, but starting his kick. Tom used some hill muscles for the first time in the race as the course intersected Park Street.

Chris was still hanging on to his international competitors, but was just about to give in and slow down when he felt a gentle touch on his shoulder, followed by a quick push on his back. The push from his father was all he needed to pull out everything he had left. Father and son became a team. As Chris went by Dylan on the left with power, Tom smoothly accelerated beside Dylan on the right.

Neither noticed that the long haired competitor made one more lunge to bump Tom, and missed. This time Dylan's legs were so tired he couldn't correct, and he hit the pavement skidding to the outside. With strength and dignity, Tom and Chris bounded to the finish, and crossed with hands held high.

In that moment, Tom's 28 year preoccupation with running, as competition only, came to an end and got a new start at the sametime. A unique sense of satisfaction shot through the father like electrcity. His feeling of self-worth was not tied to the finish place or time.

Suzi and Sam were into the first mile, running a minute and walking 2 minutes. Just as they entered the Buckhead area, they passed a large billboard which said, in big letters, "Congratulations Peachtree-ers." The greeting was signed by Phidippides.

A woman with a definite southern accent called Suzi's name and passed the twosome during a walking break, saying, "Now y'all don't run too hard now, ya hear."

Sam recognized her from the Piedmont Hospital Race. "Isn't that your roomate of last year, Suzi?"

"And Dylan's new roommate, until he finds someone else."

Sam loved the festivities. All of the major radio stations were running promotions.

Going downhill was easy for Sam and they cruised, walking one minute and running 3-4 minutes. When Sam started puffing going across the Peachtree Creek bridge, they slowed down to 2 minutes each of walking and running. Even the toughest part of the course, the big Piedmont Hospital hill was manageable for Sam. Suzi got excited as they approached the top of the hill, and whispered that they were about to pass her former roomate, who was struggling and sweating so much that her mascara was running down her face.

Suzi was from Ohio and you couldn't mistake her Midwestern twang However, she couldn't resist doing her best Scarlett O'Hara as they passed. "Now y'all don't run too hard now, ya hear." There was only the blank stare of a magnolia face accented with black stripes.

The distance between the Arts Center and Colony Square seemed to be immanant, partly because Sam was sweating profusely. Suzi was hot and wished she could sweat more. When they saw the water station at Colony square, Sam and Suzi waded through the sea of smashed cups, the army of swarming participants, and swam like salmon going upstream. Sam poured three cups on his head, and Suzi poured two. They looked like drowned rats, but felt revived.

A radio station had set up a remote broadcasting unit right at the left turn off Peachtree. Sam and Suzi had to laugh at the big sign on the radio truck: "Atlanta Beautification Project in Progress: Redneck Relocation Center."

The water station had wet the road, and the morning sun turned 14th street into gold, with dancing bodies moving with purpose toward the fulfillment of their dreams. Sam had never been as tired, or as strong and confident, as he got ready to move off his walking break.

Glancing through the tribe ahead, he was amazed to spot the one person coming back that he wanted to see at this stage of the race, his department head. As he and Suzi got back into their smoothest running form, Sam passed saying, "Now Dr.Palmer, don't get yourself in over your head." The look of amazement on his boss's face was worth the experience.

While Sam had run into Piedmont Park over a dozen times in training, he was not prepared for the emotional experience. The layers of spectators with their colorful outfits, and the roar of the crowd in all areas of the park.brought tears to his eyes. "We've come home", he told Suzi, "we've come back home."

As he reflected on his change from lying in the hospital bed, 4 months ago in the heart center, Sam started to fill with emotion. The culmination of a hard-won success had connected him with the ancient peoples in a way he'd never experienced before. "We've joined the ranks of the heros," he said.

But the normally very stoic southern gentleman found himself crying when he saw a father and a son running toward them. Tom and Chris congratulated them with the age old accolade of support and respect, the hand on the shoulder.Tom and Suzi felt totally accepted as athletes and the quartet ran through the cheering crowd as if they were the members of an elite tribe, each of whom had earned the rights of passage. The bond between them had been forged through a war, even if it was an internal one.

"The tribes are coming home," said Sam as he enjoyed feeling exhausted and felt the continued flow of energy of wave after wave of Peachtree-ers who were earning their 'hero stripes'. And the tears continued to stream down his cheeks.

"No, I haven't taken the shirt off," said Suzi. Well, to take a shower, I guess—I can't remember whether I did or not."

"Take a shower, or take the shirt off!" kidded Tom.

"It doesn't matter", clarified Sam. "My wife asked me what reward I wanted and there was only one powerful thought, to have my shirt mounted and placed in this highest point of honor. This has truly become my laurel wreath of victory. When I see it, it brings back the meaningful struggle, the dedication I thought I didn't have.

"You folks must have gotten a different shirt than the one I got. Mine just smells like perspiration," said Tom, bringing things down to earth.

Chris had joined the trio in front of Phidippides, as they framed their experiences by a toast of bagels. .

"I knew I'd find you people here," said Crazy Jim who appeared from the direction of the bagel shop. "Suzi, what's this about you moving out of your office? You move, and my clients won't

be able to find you."

Suzi laughed. "Yea, and I'd get a few more hours of sleep."

"The fact is, Suzi, you have given these people about the only sense of respect that they've had in their lives."

"But, Crazy Jim, I can't maintain the rent on my place, when I'm losing 25% of my income."

"Who said you're losing it? The State of Georgia just picked them up."

Jim explained how federal funding for these types of programs is probably gone forever, but some of it will be shifted to the states. When pressed by Suzi, to explain how he did it, a sly smile came over Jim's face.

"Lets just say that there are a number of people down at the Capitol who, say, feel guilty about one thing or another. Sometimes guilt, when it is in the hands of a legal artist, can create wonderful things."

Suzi tried to give Jim a hug, but he was already reporting on his next case, telling Sam that he'd tried to investigate his case with the University, but they wouldn't let him see the file on the Science Foundation grant he had received for his research. He was going to get back and do some work on the internet, to see what was going on.

"So Chris, what you going to do now?" asked Sam.

"I've got to try the marathon. My Dad and I have a grudge match in Portland or Twin Cities, or maybe somewhere closer like Charlotte. It's time to see who's the real man!"

"We haven't told you but Chris ran with the eventual winner of the race He gave Chris the supreme compliment. He said that when he was ready to settle for a top 10 finish, Chris challenged him, and got his competitive juices going. Chris wants to see how far he can go with his running, no promises, just a dream."

"No, a VISION," corrected Chris.

Tom said he was excited about helping to pace Chris through workouts and the early part of races. Chris confessed that he needed lots of help in this area.

"It wasn't until 24 hours after crossing that finish line," said Sam, "that I realized that I could get hooked on this. I don't know whether I'll do the marathon but I now know that I need the challenge. That scares me, but it's what I need right now. I'm dependent on thesupport. I went to Phidippides yesterday and signed up for the Galloway Marathon program."

"How do y'all cope with the reality that we are all lesser people than we used to be?" asked Sam.

They argued over who should get the fat loss award. Should it be based upon total pounds, percent of body fat lost, as a percentage of total weight, or a host of other statistical tricks which would give one the edge over the other. Everyone agreed that Chris was the loser, he was skinny to begin with. Otherwise, it was a tie. They all won. Tom asked Suzi what kept her at the same weight for two and a half months, and then allowed her to lose 14 pounds in the last 6 weeks.

"I hate to admit this, but it was the cheese. I have always loved cheese, and I went into denial about the quantity I was eating. But when I saw you two get thinner, I decided to eat fat-free cheese. At first, it tasted like it was fat-free, but then I found a couple of brands which tasted OK. Oh, yea, I also changed from low fat salad dressing to no-fat dressing. I couldn't believe that 'low fat' dressing had 90% of the calories in fat. That is very deceptive."

"I was dead set on running Peachtree, just to show someone that I could do it," Suzi continued. "But I will admit that I kept asking myself, what difference will it make if I don't run. After going through a wide range of negative counter- measures, such as 'I'll get fatter than I am', I came up with what Sam has been telling us all along. We are programmed to improve ourselves, if we can, just get the process started. When I merely attempted to do this, I felt that I was putting into motion some other positive things inside me. Even before I saw any weight loss, I was beginning to feel more control over my life, and to have more respect for myself. Running is one of those basic life experiences which activates a still undefined internal connectionthat gives us the capabilities to improve attitude, and allows access to the internal resources which can make things happen.

"I didn't feel this way before I started on this program, but, again, Sam is right. The human psyche is programmed to improve itself with the right stimulation. When we have the physical and mental structure and challenge in a program like ours, we have the best opportunity to become stable, productive and healthy persons. When we reject this process we set up a negative mental enviroment for neuroses, and other unhealthy mental conditions.

"I underestimated the powerful effect of the enjoyment and the sheer pleasure of slow running and walking," said Tom. After almost 30 years of gutting it out, assuming that there would be many bad days, I now realize that there doesn't have to be a single bad day as long as I remember to slow down.

Suzi and Tom asked Sam if the Peachtree experience affected his outlook on the job situation at the University.

"Throughout this Spring, I felt the rumblings of self-confidence inside me. This affected my ability to cope with the professional change which I had been denying. Running gave me a mental cleaning out. It dampened the effects of the stress while and at the same time encouraged the re-birth of a person with

self-confidence and high self-esteem. When the reality hit, and I was told that my job was gone, it temporarily took away the only real source of satisfaction I had on a daily basis. I didn't realize that the seeds of my emotional rebirth were already planted.

"But I was so depressed that I couldn't exercise. Things got worse and there didn't seem to be a way out. Ironically, I did turn to running as a solution to my problem, albeit a perverted solution. In a way, it worked. It got me the personal attention I desperately needed at the time.

"These misguided hill sessions accelerated the confidence rebuildng which I needed. As I did what I thought were heart-busting hill workouts, I started to feel more and more secure again. By the time I collapsed on the hill, I was ready to move on. I was stronger outside and inside, except for being dehydrated.

"But I'm more ready now than ever to move to the next level. As they used to say back in Mt. Airy, 'You're dam-right'. I'm ready for the challenge of the marathon. I might only end up with the half marathon, but I've already sent in my application to the Galloway marathon group. It's wonderful to have a choice."

Just then, a long-haired figure huffed and puffed his way from behind and joined them. Suzi made the mistake of saying that she could tell it was crazy Jim by his heavy breathing, which inspired several comments. Jim announced that he had some news for Sam.

"Sam, I've finally confirmed the facts of your grant. First, it was originally written in your name, not the university. Second, the university tried to get the name of the grant tranferred over to the university, and the Science Foundation wouldn't allow it. And now the big bombshell. The NSF has renewed it for another 10 years, and funded every area you asked for—the research in Greece, the treadmill studies, etc. Not only does the University have to sign the grant over to you, it is liable for punitive damages.

"The bottom line is that you can take your grant elsewhere and set up your own lab, or you can carve out a great facility at the University."

Sam didn't have to think long before replying: "It's great to have a choice."

"What about Dylan, Suzi? You haven't even mentioned him," said Tom.

"After so many years of building my relationship life around him, I was bitter for about a month after I saw him with my two-faced roommate. I'm also convinced that if I didn't have this great physical, mental and emotional challenge and support from you guys, that I would still be dwelling on that negative situation. When I became a runner, through Peachtree, I moved into a new consciousness level. The process involved me socompletely that I came out of the negativism with the bigger picture:

- that these things happen to everyone

- that it is totally unproductive to deal with the fact that "he done me wrong"
- to do so only gives him more control over me
- that the transformation power of endurance exercise is stronger than any therapy I know
- that I have real power inside of me to deal with problems and make changes

"I have a theory on this," continued Suzi. "Endurance walking/running/cruising is such a positive activity for the body and mind that we are already wired for positive responses in every area, if we just get out there regularly. Through my team-supported Peachtree program, I wiped my negative slate clean and am ready to embrace the positive.

"Did you see Dylan afterwards?" asked Sam.

"I guess I can take time for one last negative thought. I hadn't seen him, even during the awards ceremony. As I was walking towards Phidippides to meet up with you guys, there he was, almost shouting at (her). He was berating her for not finishing the race. I shouted his name. He looked and I pointed to my shirt. The look on his face was worth every drop of sweat I've lost."

"I was behind you," added Sam. "You didn't hear this, but he said as you left 'I don't care who passes you. You're an unbelieveable wimp for not finishing.'"

"How do you psychologically classify

the chuckles you're expressing right now?" asked Tom.

"Totally designed to let off steam and unrelated to vindictiveness. Well,.a little retribution every once in a while is good for the soul."

"Until I went through this," Sam explained, "I wondered why the ancients so tenaciously clung to every detail of their rituals and ceremonies. Now I know that they were continually doing 'urban renewal' on their belief environment. Everything had to have a place, whether it made sense or not. Most of them probably experienced the simple truth that everything can be connected. This became clearer to me after the Peachtree."

"It's not the laurel weath but the pursuit of it. It's not the experience but the challenge expected. Running is not a miracle or the only way to develop these things but it engages the organism, connecting enough of the components and supplying the energy to make it happen."

"And it's one of the only 'total' ways to have fun," added Tom.

Back trails...and background on the author

The summer I turned 14 was a period of great change in my life. My family moved from a comfortable, laid-back community in Florida to the busy, ambitious, and competitive environment of Atlanta. The change provide me with a heritage of wonderful opportunities that I wouldn't have had in Green Cove Springs. It was the end of a cozy chapter in my life, and beginning of the struggle into adulthood.

That summer, I started running. Initially, I joined the track and cross country teams to fulfill a high school requirement that all boys participate in a sport of choice. It took only a few weeks, however, for me to realize that I had found a refuge. Running offered and developed an internal support structure that helped sort out the many adolescent questions which were spinning inside. Daily runs, blended some childish humor and energy, led me to journeys into the right brain, which I have found so valuable (and entertaining) as an adult. Regardless of the other insecurities which raced through my psyche, running always

bestowed a mental boost and a positive structure around which I could organize the other components of my life.

I was an overweight child, and had developed an image of myself as obese. It took two decades to complete erase this image. While I did not like my physical shape or condition before and during my first year of running, I was comfortable with it. While I intuitively knew that the exercise was producing a wide range of positive changes, for almost 20 years I lived with the fear that my fat body when I reduced the amount of running I was doing. During every injury hiatus, I could almost feel the fat grams accumulating around my middle, turning me into my original shape.

As I stripped away the layers of fat from my body, my mental processes became more direct, and more energetic. Running intuitively became an analogy for the way I conducted other areas of my life. Intuitively, I slowed the pace of most of my runs and became hooked on this positive lifestyle. Sub-consciously I understood that a run of around 45 minutes or more started opening up the creative areasof the right brain. Not only did my runs become more fun, I began to apply the creative flow to other areas of life.

The confidence I gained from having this productive contorl over mood and mind-set is one of the richest parts of my life today. To a 14 year-old, these after-run effects were magical; they bestowed needed focus to a college student, and then a Naval officer. The adult world is not as troubling when you have a stress dissolver, mind-formatter, and positive mood manager, as I have had in my running. At each level of growth, running introduced me to a group of energetic, interesting friends. But the most powerful benefit was totally unexpected. No matter what problems had been rumbling around before the run, the "afterglow" bestowed a new outlook, along with the energy to look for more solutions and possibilities. This capability has only increased through the years.

My number one hero gently led me into running, my dad. Like many boys, I wanted to be like him when I grew up. He intuitively understood my secret desire to be an athlete and matched me up with the perfect activity. But this was particlly by default. In a Green Cove Springs little league game I tried to throw a runner out at home plate, but over-achieved. The ball sailed over the backstop, the concession stands, and probably the parking lot beyond. As a 13 year old football player, I had one moment of glory headed for the goal, free and clear, except for a gutsy guy half my size. He tackled me and sent an uproar of laughter through the team and the spectators. Thankfully, my father supported my running.

But as I became more absorbed in the process of becoming fit, my father moved in the other direction. He weighed 50 pounds over the American average weight, and his negativity increased proportionally. Simultaneously, my father's activity level went down and so did my respect for him. During my twenties, it became my mission to get him into any type of fitness activity, but he always had an excuse. It was a sad point in my young adult life when I realized that my dad was no longer my hero, and I didn't have another to replace him. This was, you see, the sixties.

Without realizing it at the time, I was beginning to identify with another type of heroic individual—those in any area of life who made challenging course changes when they saw a better path. It was inspiring to learn that people in difficult situations were often able to access hidden strengths, and by developing these strengths, could make successful changes, or overcome problems. As I progressed throught the competitive world of running, I found more of these outstanding people. Each run provided the opportunity to become a hero, at least in a small way.

My years of trying to coax my father into running did absolutely no good. His inspiration came from a high school reunion, when he was 52. Out of 25 football players in his graduating class, 13 had already died of degenerative diseases. On the long drive back, Elliott Galloway realized that he could very well be the next one to die. By the time he returned from the trip, he had decided to live. The next morning he was going to run circles around the joggers who went by his office.

It wasn't that simple. The mind remembered, but the body didn't. He couldn't run from one telephone pole to the next one. Humiliated, but not defeated, he was out there again, two days later, trying to make it to the second telephone pole. A year later he made it completely around the park (3 miles). The following year he finished Atlanta's greatest energy source, the Peachtree Road Race (6.2 miles). Before he turned 60, Elliott Galloway ran a marathon (26.2 miles) in 2:59 minutes. In the process, he lost 50 pounds and gained a new positive mental outlook.

While he no longer does speedwork, my dad, who is in his mid 70's often logs more miles per week than I do. Officially "retired" from the school he founded, he "only" works an 8 hour work day. He's got a great attitude, and knows how to positively maintain his health.

He's my hero again. I hope I can be like him when I grow up.

FEEDBACK QUESTIONNAIRE

160

I need your help

This book is not finished. I need your help in modifying, extending and improving it. If you have suggestions which are not covered by this questionnaire, please use a separate piece of paper.

Thanks!
Jeff Galloway

Which topics and specific areas need to be expanded and explained?

_____

_____

_____

What topics and areas would you like to see covered—which are not now covered?

_____

_____

_____

Any suggestions for the story itself? _____

_____

_____

_____

What would you recommend for a sequel? _____

_____

_____

Any specific questions which I could answer? _____

_____

_____

Please include your name and we will send you occasional updates and other fitness news

Name _____

Address _____

Phone _____

Fax_____ E-mail _____

ATLANTA
OFFICE DEPOT
CORPORATE
CHALLENGE ™
Presented by
PROMINA
HEALTH
SYSTEM

To recieve
Registration
material call:
404/255-1033
ext.12

Thursday, September 28, 1995
6:45 P.M.
The Olympic Stadium
Directed Nationally by Jeff Galloway
Produced by Phidippides Runners/Galloway Productions

* Part of the Chemical Bank Corporaye Challenge Series. Corporate Challenge is a
Registered Trademark of Chemical Bank

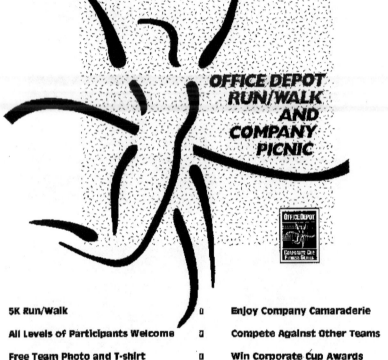

OFFICE DEPOT RUN/WALK AND COMPANY PICNIC

- 5K Run/Walk
- All Levels of Participants Welcome
- Free Team Photo and T-shirt

- Enjoy Company Camaraderie
- Compete Against Other Teams
- Win Corporate Cup Awards

Atlanta
Chicago
Dallas/Ft. Worth
Denver
Detroit
Houston

Office DEPOT
OFFICE DEPOT
CORPORATE CUP FITNESS SERIES

Portland
San Diego
San Francisco
Seattle
Washington, D.C.

For Information and Registration Materials
Call 1-800-200-2771 or Fax 404-252-3971
Directed Nationally by Jeff Galloway

BREAKING THE TAPE

RUNNING WITH
JEFF GALLOWAY

THE COMPLETE RUNNING TRAINER IN A BOX WILL HELP YOU RUN BETTER! FASTER! LONGER!

Breaking the Tape is based on the World Famous training ideas and principals of the current best selling author on running - Jeff Galloway. Jeff helps runners - no matter what level - set up and maintain their running training program, reach their personal fitness goals - and discover a healthy running lifestyle!

This program comes with two 30-minute VHS videotapes. The first tape has tips on nutrition, stretching, choosing the right shoes, running injury-free and cross training. The second tape displays tips on form, pacing and peaking, setting realistic goals, building an interval speedwork plan and training for the 5K and 10K. It even includes Jeff's 6 month world famous marathon program!

You can also purchase....
The Complete Running Trainer in a Box
This program is "complete" with two 30-minute VHS videotapes, a motivational audio cassette and personal performance journal.

Yes, please send

____	Breaking the Tape	$15.95
____	Complete Running Trainer in a Box	$20.95

Please add $3.75 for shipping and handling costs.

NAME _____

ADDRESS _____

CITY, STATE, ZIP _____

Please mail order to:
Galloway Productions
PO BOX 720182
Atlanta, GA 30358

166

NOTES

NOTES

NOTES

NOTES

NOTES

NOTES

NOTES

NOTES

NOTES

NOTES

NOTES

NOTES

NOTES

NOTES

NOTES

NOTES